I0671746

Brew Confessions

HEDGEWITCH FOR HIRE – BOOK 11

CHRISTINE POPE

This is a work of fiction. Names, characters, places, and incidents are either the product of the author's imagination or are used fictitiously. Any resemblance to actual events, places, organizations, or persons, whether living or dead, is entirely coincidental.

BREW CONFESSIONS

Copyright © 2024 by Christine Pope

Published by Dark Valentine Press

ISBN: 978-1-946435-70-5

Cover design by Lou Harper

Ebook formatting by Indie Author Services

All rights reserved. No part of this book may be reproduced in any form or by any electronic or mechanical means, including information storage and retrieval systems—except in the case of brief quotations embodied in critical articles or reviews—without permission in writing from its publisher, Dark Valentine Press.

ONE

Holly Jolly

JOSIE WOODROW BREEZED INTO MY SHOP at a little past ten that Monday morning, looking festive as usual. With Christmas only ten days off, she was obviously already in the spirit, wearing a scarlet blazer that clashed wildly with her bright orange-red hair, a blazer accented with a holiday tree pin with varicolored rhinestones that glittered on one lapel. In one hand, she held an oversized flyer.

"Hi, Selena," she said, her tone cheerful. "I was wondering if you wouldn't mind putting this in your shop window."

Since I was always happy to accommodate most of Josie's schemes—as Globe's mayor she was usually plotting some sort of attraction or event to boost the town's profile and bring in more visitors —I took the flyer from her and glanced down at its contents. Feeling my welcoming smile beginning to fade, I read out loud, "'High Country Holiday Brewing Competition'?"

"Yes," she said, either not noticing or deciding to ignore the distinct lack of enthusiasm in my tone. "I thought it would be the perfect thing to get everyone in the holiday spirit!"

I'd never thought of beer as being a particularly Christmas-y beverage, but then again, I'd be the first to admit I wasn't much of a beer drinker, even before I'd gotten pregnant. Now, at nearly six months along, I was jonesing for a margarita or a glass of wine like a fiend, but those alcohol cravings hadn't extended to a tall glass of lager.

However, if Josie wanted to host a brewing competition here in town, I was all for it. No, my current worry that she might have bitten off more than she could chew only centered around the timing of the whole thing, and not the substance of the event itself.

"This is only five days away," I pointed out as I set the flyer down on the counter. Because Josie had come in right after opening, I hadn't had time to retreat to the stool I'd set up behind the cash register so I could rest my feet during the slow times. No, I wasn't huge yet—my fears that the baby I was carrying would take after my six-foot-five husband hadn't materialized, and I was still able to squeeze into some non-maternity clothes as long as they weren't jeans—but I tried to give my feet and back a rest whenever things were slow at the shop.

"Oh, I know," Josie said, giving one of her patented airy hand waves, the kind of gesture she generally employed whenever she wanted to brush aside issues she didn't think were of any particular concern. "But I've actually been working on this behind the scenes for a while. I just didn't want to get out there and start advertising it until I had all the brewers lined up."

"'All'?" I echoed as I wondered exactly how involved this competition was going to be. My brain conjured images of bearded hipsters in man buns descending on Globe, ready to share their latest hoppy concoctions with the world.

For the first time, Josie appeared just slightly less than supremely confident. "Well, there are only six of them, as it turns out," she confessed. "I couldn't get any more than that to agree to participate, since a lot of people already had holiday plans. But still, they're some of the best brewers in the Southwest. It's going to be a wonderful competition."

All right, a half dozen brewers sounded a little less overwhelming than the horde I'd first imagined. At the same time, though, I couldn't think of many places in my adopted hometown that could accommodate the sort of function Josie had apparently planned. We had a couple of bars and a lovely little winery on the eastern edge of town, but no brewpubs, no other locations that were the kind of venue that would work for Josie's impromptu tournament.

"Where are you going to host the competition?" I asked, genuinely curious.

Looking relieved that I apparently wasn't going to ask any more probing questions about the viability of such a last-minute event, Josie responded, "Oh, at the old high school. The gymnasium is the perfect place for the brewers to set up their booths, and they'll have access to the kitchen whenever they need it."

The former high school sat at the end of Broad Street, the same downtown avenue where my own shop was located. Ever since I'd moved to town, the big building—built in the 1930s with WPA labor—had sat empty. It had been abandoned back in the early 1990s when the new, much more modern high school opened to some fanfare, and ever since then, no one seemed to know what to do with the older facility. From time to time, it had served as the site of various craft fairs and other events that needed indoor space, and sort of functioned as the town's unofficial convention center.

"That sounds like a good idea," I said, and Josie nodded, now looking pleased that I seemed to be on board with her plan.

"It was the first thing that sprang to my mind when I started planning the competition," she told me. "I'm just glad we've continued to allocate some funds to the old high school's upkeep so it hasn't deteriorated too badly. Brett's there now, working on upgrading the electrical in the gymnasium so the brewers can run all their equipment, and he's also building little display areas for all six of them."

Brett Woodrow was Josie's nephew. His contractor skills kept him in high demand around town, so I was a little surprised he'd been available on such short notice. I commented on that fact, and Josie only smiled.

"He had a job scheduled for this week, but they canceled at the last minute...something about the funding for their second mortgage falling through," she said. "That's why he was available. To me, it seems like the universe got everything lined up exactly the way it was supposed to be."

Since I myself held the philosophy that the universe often guided us in exactly such a way, I didn't bother to argue with her remark. Instead, I only said, "That does sound like a stroke of luck. And you were able to find places for everyone to stay?"

Because, although Globe had several Airbnbs —including one owned by my best friend, Hazel Marr—and one decent hotel, we were also getting close enough to the holidays that I didn't see how

Josie would have been able to locate lodging for everyone in the competition at such short notice.

"I did," she said. "Hazel's putting up one of them in her Airbnb, and the rest are staying in Mavis's places."

Josie's friend Mavis was sort of an Airbnb mogul in Globe, since she had owned four homes for years and recently picked up another one just a month or so earlier. I could see why Josie would want the brewing competition's contestants to be staying in houses rather than a hotel, but I was a little surprised that Mavis had been able to accommodate all of them. Usually, her vacation rentals were booked months in advance.

"I reached out to her a while back and asked her to keep her rentals open for me," Josie explained, probably in response to the questioning look on my face. "Since we're such old friends, she didn't have a problem with that."

Holding all those Airbnbs back during such a busy season still seemed like kind of a big ask— from what I could tell, the final plans for the competition had only just fallen into place within the last few days—but I wasn't going to probe too deeply. It seemed clear enough that our esteemed mayor had held her cards pretty close to the vest on this one, and had only divulged her scheme to the parties involved in case the whole thing fell apart and she was left with egg on her face.

As to who was paying for all those rentals, I didn't know. It was possible that Josie was covering the whole thing out of pocket. Her real estate business did very well, and since her house had been paid off for years, I knew she didn't have a lot of overhead.

And while I might have been irked with my friend Hazel for not telling me what was going on, I guessed that Josie had sworn her to secrecy, and I had to respect that. Hazel and I had been friends almost since the time I moved to Globe, and I knew she would never hold something back unless she'd been expressly directed to keep quiet.

"So, when are all the brewers arriving?" I asked next, since that seemed like an innocent enough question.

"Most of them are getting here on Thursday," Josie replied, her relieved expression telling me she was glad I hadn't kept probing at the logistics behind the competition and exactly who was funding everything. "In fact, we're going to have a reception Thursday night to welcome them all here. Then on Friday, they'll work on setting up their booths at the old high school, and on Saturday, the judging will begin."

"Who're the judges?"

Because whoever they were, they'd also stayed completely silent on the subject of the High Country Holiday Brewing Competition.

"Oh, Chuck," Josie replied at once. I probably shouldn't have been surprised; Hazel's husband Chuck Langdon was a big fan of craft brews. "And Brett...and Henry Lewis."

The identity of the final judge startled me. True, it wasn't as if I hung out with the police chief on a regular basis—although we had gotten friendlier as the years had gone by, thanks in no small part to the efforts of his wife Joyce, whose candles I sold at my store—but I supposed I'd never thought of him as much of a beer drinker.

"Henry's never on duty on the weekends," Josie went on, probably trying to fill the surprised silence that followed her revelation. "Otherwise, he wouldn't have agreed to be a judge. But he's been brewing his own beer at home for years now, so I thought that made him a logical person to sit on the panel."

Again, news to me. However, it wasn't as though Henry and I had ever sat down for lunch together and had a cozy chat about our various hobbies. He probably knew I read Tarot cards and employed a pendulum from time to time, just because I'd used those ritual tools to help me solve the various murders that had taken place around Globe over the past few years, but still, it wasn't as though we'd ever shared our life secrets.

"That does make sense," I agreed.

"And you'll come to the reception, won't you?"

Josie asked then, her tone now a little anxious. "I know you won't be able to have any champagne or anything, but—"

"It's fine," I assured her. By that point, I was used to standing around with a glass of water or sparkling cider on special occasions while everyone else indulged, so I didn't have a problem with watching the rest of the guests at the reception drink their favorite form of bubbly, whether that was champagne or beer. "I can be there. And Calvin, too—luckily, he's not working Thursday night."

"Perfect," Josie said, her round face practically glowing with relief. "You're one of our most prominent business owners, so it wouldn't have felt right to not have you there."

I wasn't sure about "prominent"—my friend Archie's dance studio next door was doing very well, and the art gallery down the street where Hazel displayed a lot of her paintings was also a favorite destination in Globe's tiny downtown— but I didn't argue. "It sounds like fun," I said. "Just let me know if you need any help with anything."

"Oh, it's all handled," Josie assured me. "I've hired a caterer, and Mavis is helping me with the decor. I'll bring around the formal invitation later today."

That really didn't seem necessary, not when Josie had already told me about the reception and

I'd agreed to come, but I only nodded. It seemed clear enough that she had a mental checklist she wanted to follow, so I'd go along with her if it made her happy.

With Calvin's and my presence at the reception settled, Josie reminded me to put the flyer in the shop's front window and said goodbye before sailing outside. The day was gray and lowering, although no snow had been forecast. Still, I was a little surprised that she hadn't bothered to put on a coat or even a wrap of some kind.

Then again, Josie generated her own kind of energy. She never seemed to get cold in the winter or hot in the summer.

My hand rested on the swell of my belly, and I couldn't help smiling. I was very glad I'd be at my biggest during the coldest months, because even now, I got overheated if the temperature indoors even began to inch over sixty-eight degrees. Luckily, most people who came into my shop were bundled up from walking around outside, so no one seemed to mind that it wasn't exactly warm and cozy inside the store.

Still smiling, I picked up the flyer Josie had given me, got some tape from under the counter, and headed over to attach it to the front window of my store.

"I see you're in the know now," Hazel told me later that afternoon when she dropped in to check on me. Lately, she'd been helping out on Fridays and Saturdays, the two busiest days at Once in a Blue Moon, but it was clear she'd come by this Monday mainly to talk about the brewing competition.

"I am," I said with a grin. "It must have been killing you to keep all this secret."

"Well, I don't know about 'killing,'" Hazel said as she returned my smile. Like me, she was in her early thirties, although her hair was a light brown in contrast to my near-black tresses, and she had gold-flecked greenish eyes that perfectly matched her name. "But I'm glad that now I don't have to worry about letting the wrong thing slip. Josie knew she was kind of taking a chance with this brewing competition, so she wanted to make sure everything was in place before she started publicizing it."

"And you really think she's going to get that many people here on such late notice?" I asked.

Hazel shrugged. Unlike Josie, she was wearing a puffer coat, this one in a shade of pea green that only Hazel could pull off, although she'd unzipped it as she came into the shop. "It sounds like a lot of the brewers have their own followings, and since each of them came up with a new brew for the competition, they want to be here to taste it."

I supposed that made sense. Still....

"And they're going to make the beer here?" I said. "I'll admit I don't know much about it, but I thought that took a lot longer than a couple of days."

My friend's gold-green eyes glinted with amusement at my ignorance. Not that I'd ever suspected Hazel of being an expert in all things beer, but I guessed Chuck had probably explained a few things to her.

"Oh, they're not making it on site," she replied. "I mean, it sounds like they're going to have some kind of vat at each of their stations as part of the display, but the beer's already been made and bottled. I guess they're supposed to bring two cases each, and some will be for the judging and the rest will be sold to the attendees of the competition. It's twenty-five bucks just to get in, so a lot of money will be raised that way. I'm not tracking any of it, but Josie made it sound as if online ticket sales have been pretty brisk even though she just started them yesterday, and she's expecting to be sold out at least for Saturday by the end of the week."

This was all news to me. However, since my time online had been spent mainly on shopping for things for the nursery and picking out baby clothes, I supposed I could be forgiven for completely missing the news that Globe was going to be hosting a brewing competition in mid-

December, especially since the tickets had only gone on sale the day before.

"It all sounds great," I said, and Hazel nodded.

"Yes, Josie's hoping the competition will generate enough interest in Globe that we might finally be able to have a brewpub here. It's great to have the winery, but some people really aren't into that kind of thing."

I had to agree that having a brewpub would probably be an additional draw for Globe's downtown. "Where was she thinking of?" I asked. "The old hardware store?"

Not that it had been a hardware store for the three-plus years I'd been living here. No, it was just a big, empty building across the street and halfway down the block, a place with a perpetual "For Sale" sign on its dusty storefront windows.

But the location was great, and it definitely had the square footage. And I had to believe Josie would be all too glad to finally sell a property that had been sitting on her books for years.

"That's the one," Hazel said. "In fact, it sounds like one of the competitors—a guy named Trent Reynolds—is already interested, although he wants to see how things go this weekend before he makes any commitments."

"Fair enough," I replied. Although it had been kind of a brash move for me to buy the store and the apartment above it sight unseen, I could understand why this Trent person would want to wait and evaluate how much interest there really was in a brewpub in Globe before he sank any of his own money into the venture.

"And you're coming to the reception, right?" Hazel asked next, now sounding a little anxious. I got the feeling Josie expected her to be there, but that Hazel would feel better about the whole thing if she had a couple of her friends accompanying her.

"Absolutely," I said, and, while she didn't exactly let out a breath of relief, I could tell by the way her shoulders relaxed a little that she was very glad I hadn't begged off from the event. "I need to talk to Calvin about it, but I don't see any reason why he wouldn't want to go."

"Perfect," Hazel said. "I need to pop into Sundowner—Don sold another of my paintings and I have to pick up the check—but I wanted to make sure Josie had talked to you. She told me she would, but you know how busy she gets sometimes."

I said that I did, and then offered a wave as Hazel rezipped her puffer jacket and headed back outside. We'd see each other Thursday night, of course, and again on Friday when she came to help out at the store. The holiday shopping season was in full swing, and I definitely needed her assistance on those busy weekend days.

Deep down, I knew I needed to start looking for full-time help, but something in me balked at taking that step. My last experience with hiring a shop assistant had ended in disaster, since the woman who'd come to work for me had turned out to be a blackmailer...and a stone-cold killer to boot. Once upon a time, my ability to view auras might have helped me see the blackness in her soul, but the half-shifter baby I carried inside me had been effectively blocking that talent, and I hadn't discovered Melanie Knowles' true self until it was almost too late.

Fortunately, the auras had mostly come back, and the brain fog and confusion of those days seemed to have dissipated as well. I couldn't say I didn't experience "pregnancy brain" every once in a while, but I generally felt like my normal self. And since the auras had never been one hundred percent reliable—they came and went at their own whim, and definitely not at my command—I supposed I should be glad I could still see them from time to time.

After the first of the year, I told myself. At this point, there didn't seem to be much reason to hire someone when we were only two weeks away from Christmas. I was getting by just fine with Hazel's help, and after the holidays, things would be quiet enough that I should have no problem focusing on getting a decent shop assistant who could take over for me when I went on maternity leave in early March.

At least, that was the plan.

In the meantime, though, the brewing competition seemed like an innocent enough diversion, something to help everyone get even more in the holiday spirit. If Globe's downtown gained a brewpub out of it, all the better. I loved my adopted hometown and wanted only the best for it, and that meant cheering on Josie Woodrow's latest project, even if it seemed awfully last-minute to me.

If nothing else, the contest would help distract everyone from Melanie's upcoming trial and the way she'd been arrested right here in this shop. It would be a good way to stop people from referring to Globe as the "murder capital of the Southwest," which I thought was awfully unfair. We'd had a run of bad luck, that's all.

Now if we could just convince everyone else of that.

TWO

Six of Swords

Luckily, Calvin was just fine with going to the reception, although he, too, was a little surprised by the way Josie had managed to plan the whole thing behind our backs.

"At least I thought I would've heard about it from my deputies," he told me over dinner that night. "This sounds like the kind of thing where Josie would've wanted to hire them for some extra security."

True enough. Although the San Ramon tribal police department paid its deputies fairly well, that still didn't stop some of them from moonlighting as security guards for special events like Globe's Fourth of July carnival or the big tent revival that had been held in Memorial Park two Thanksgivings ago. Of course, the off-duty officers hadn't done a very good job of protecting Aaron Galloway from the poison that Mark Lemmon had slipped into his coffee mug backstage, but I couldn't really blame them for that. They'd been there to provide general crowd control, not to keep an eye out for disgruntled husbands whose wives had spent all their life savings on the televangelist's cause.

"Maybe Josie didn't want to ask anyone to work security until she knew for sure the event was happening," I suggested, then took a bite of my Italian sausage sandwich. I'd roasted the sausage in the oven along with onions and bell peppers, and piled everything on a hoagie roll. Super-caloric, but since my pregnancy weight gain was right where my doctor wanted it to be, I wasn't too worried about indulging every once in a while. I hadn't had any stomach issues at all after I was past the nausea that came and went during my first trimester, so I could eat pretty much what I wanted.

Calvin nodded. "That makes sense. Also, Josie couldn't really schedule them too far ahead anyway, since we don't work out the duty roster any earlier than a week in advance."

Which sometimes could be a real pain if you were trying to plan anything major. As the chief of the tribal police, my husband had a little more leeway when it came to moving his schedule around, although he did his best not to abuse the privilege. And lately, he'd been working a lot of nights and weekends so he wouldn't cause too much resentment when he went to a strict week-day, eight-to-five schedule after the baby came. He was already planning to take a month off for parental leave, but the department really couldn't afford to spare him for any longer than that.

"I guess you shouldn't be too surprised if a couple of your deputies end up working the event," I said. "Now that it looks as if everything's falling into place, I assume Josie will want the extra secu-rity. Or at least, I'd think she would."

Calvin had just taken a bite of his sandwich, so I had to wait for him to finish chewing before he could reply. "Probably. It sounds like they're going to be selling alcohol at the competition, which means she'll need more security guards than she might for a dry event."

"You really think people are going to get all crazy at a holiday brewing contest?" I asked, my tone wry, but his expression remained serious.

"You'd be surprised. Anyway, it just makes sense to take the necessary precautions."

I had to hope Josie's event wouldn't turn into a drunken brawl. No, what I hoped was that there would be a sell-out crowd, and a fun, lively contest to spark interest in the brewers of the Southwest and...with any luck...lead to this Trent Reynolds person deciding Globe seemed pretty neat after all and would be the perfect place for his new brewpub.

Fingers crossed.

Thursday evening rolled around, still chilly, although the clouds had cleared out and there didn't seem to be any threat of snow. Because we were coming from opposite sides of town, there was no reason for Calvin and me to drive to the reception with Hazel and Chuck, although I'd promised her earlier via text that we would be there right on time at seven o'clock.

We'd eaten a light meal before we left the house, since it sounded as though this was going to be an *hors d'oeuvres* and drinks kind of thing and not a real dinner. Luckily, I'd already bought a pretty red dress with a high waist in anticipation of wearing it at Christmas, so I'd put that on, along with my favorite pair of black knee-high boots with kitten heels and some silver and garnet jewelry I'd "borrowed" from the collection I sold at my store.

Despite my careful preparations, I couldn't help feeling obviously, conspicuously pregnant. After I climbed into Calvin's Tahoe and labored to buckle my seatbelt, I complained, "I look like a complete whale."

"The world's most beautiful whale," he replied as he started the engine, and I sent him some serious side-eye.

"That's not funny."

"I didn't mean it as a joke," he said. "You're beautiful no matter what, Selena. Actually, you look especially beautiful right now. You've got that whole glowing earth-mother thing going on."

Well, maybe I would keep him after all. Smiling, I leaned over and pressed a kiss against his cheek, and he grinned even while backing out of the driveway. After some gentle nudging—all right, some outright nagging—I'd gotten him to clear out enough of the garage so I could park my Jeep Renegade inside. However, the other half remained full of boxes, tools, and unidentified junk, so he had to continue to park his San Ramon tribal police SUV outside.

I supposed that was between him and the San Ramon P.D., since they were the ones who supplied his official-issue Durango. They didn't seem to have a problem with him driving it all the time, even when he wasn't on duty, probably because he was almost always on call and had to show up at any serious enough crime scenes, no matter what hour of the day or night it might be.

Luckily, that didn't happen very often. Most of the time, his job seemed to consist of keeping an eye out for people speeding through the tribal lands or having a few too many drinks at the Gold Dust casino, which the San Ramon Apache operated and used as the main source of income for the tribe. There was also the occasional marauding cow to deal with, but except for a few scary moments a couple of years ago when Calvin and some of his deputies had to bust up a meth lab that was operating just inside his jurisdiction, his work didn't seem to put him in harm's way too often.

No, an outside observer might have noted I was the one in danger far more often, even though I certainly didn't have a career in law enforcement.

However, since the debacle with Melanie Knowles had occurred only a few weeks ago, I had to believe things should be uneventful for the next couple of months. We'd have a cozy holiday, since my mother and her husband Tom were coming out to visit the day after Christmas and planned to stay through New Year's, and after that would be what I always thought of as the dead time of the year, those quiet weeks after the holidays and before Valentine's Day rolled around.

We pulled into the parking lot at the old high school just as Hazel and Chuck drove up in his gleaming black Chevy Silverado. Although I'd seen him driving the truck around his ranch, hauling hay and whatnot, it was still hard to believe that he actually used it for such mundane chores, since it always looked as shiny and clean as though he'd just driven it off the lot.

Because this was an evening event, they'd both dressed up a little, with Chuck wearing a jacket over his plaid shirt and Hazel in an actual dress, although she had a shawl wrapped around her shoulders to protect her from the chilly December night air. She gave me a little wave as she climbed out of the truck, obviously taking extra care because she, like me, wore heeled boots rather than her usual flats or tennis shoes.

I'd always gotten the impression that it would take an act of God to pry Chuck out of his cowboy boots, and sure enough, he was wearing the same brown ones he seemed to have on no matter what the time of year or the occasion. However, it appeared as though he'd polished them as a nod to the sort of event we were about to attend.

After we exchanged greetings, Hazel commented, "I'm really interested to see what Brett and Josie have cooked up for the gymnasium. I've been to a couple of craft shows here, and it never seemed like the kind of place that would work for what she was planning."

I had to agree with Hazel on that point. Not too long after I'd moved to Globe, I'd gone to one of those fairs as well, and although I saw a lot of cute things for sale, the gymnasium itself was just a large, cavernous space, big on room but pretty low on charm.

But Brett was an absolute genius contractor, and Josie, while not a decorator, had definitely sold enough houses over the years that she knew what worked and what didn't, and knew how to stage furniture and accessories to get the best effect. And when we bumped into our friends Archie and Victoria just as we were about to enter the gym, I had a pretty good idea who else had been involved in bringing Josie's vision to life.

"Don't tell me you were in on this, too," I said to Victoria, who had the grace to appear just slightly shamefaced.

"Well, I offered some advice," she replied, while next to her, Archie shook his head. As usual, they both looked impeccable, with Archie in a dark gray suit that seemed a little out of place for extremely informal Globe, Arizona, while Victoria had on a champagne-colored dress beneath her winter white coat. Not for the first time, I thought they could have stepped out of a scene from a movie, with their classic good looks and blond hair and blue eyes.

"If by 'advice,' you mean making up a bunch of sketches and going shopping with Josie in Phoenix to get all the supplies she needed," Archie remarked, the corners of his mouth quirking, "then yes, that's exactly what Victoria provided."

His wife's shoulders lifted in a graceful shrug. "Well, I was done with the Mariposa Heights project, and my next one won't start until after the first of the year, so it's not as though I didn't have the time."

Mariposa Heights was a largish housing development that had just completed construction on the eastern edge of town. Or rather, the model homes and the first ten houses were now built, and all the homesites and streets neatly laid out. Since it had been Victoria's task to decorate the five model homes, she'd been busy the past few months, but now she could sit back and, if not exactly rest on her laurels, at least allow herself a little time off before she dived into the project she'd be starting in January. That one would be over in Gilbert, meaning she'd have a long commute whenever she had to go to the job site, but she'd made it sound as though she didn't think she'd have to make the drive more than once or twice a week.

Anyway, since sitting around and watching HGTV or reading romance novels to fill up her time wasn't exactly Victoria's M.O., I wasn't too surprised to learn she'd been aiding and abetting Josie and Hazel and Brett in getting the brewing competition site up and running. And, now that I knew all of them had been involved, I really wanted to see what they'd done.

"Well, let's go inside and see the fruits of your labor," Hazel put in. "It's freezing out here."

Maybe that was a slight exaggeration, but since the temperature hovered around forty degrees outside, I could see why she wanted to get into the hall and out of the cold.

Everyone was agreeable to that, so the six of us headed inside. I had to keep myself from staring in wonder, because if I hadn't known this was the old high school gymnasium, I would have thought the facility had been built especially for this purpose. Immediately to our right was a coat-check area with one of the girls from the local high school—at least, I assumed she was a student, since she didn't look much older than sixteen or seventeen at the most—taking everyone's wraps and jackets, and issuing claim tickets in return.

Directly ahead, though, was a series of small rooms open on the side facing the gym's double doors and also open to the ceiling above. Each of those rooms had a large copper vat off to one side, maybe just for decoration, since all the contestants had brought beers and lagers and ales that had been prepared earlier off-site. On the wall opposite those vats were several floating shelves that carried each brewer's wares, and each of the rooms also had a small bar, although I couldn't tell whether those were for show or whether the people attending the event would actually be able to get a drink there.

I noticed right away that each of the little chambers, or whatever you wanted to call them, had a distinctly different decor that I guessed Victoria had tailored to the individual style of each brewer. One was very modern, almost austere, while another had been decorated in a sort of farmhouse industrial style. Yet another had a shabby-chic vibe, while the one next to that wouldn't have been out of place in a Victorian home, with dark green embossed wallpaper and dark stain on the shelves.

"This is amazing," I said. "How in the world were you able to pull all this together so quickly?"

Once again, Victoria gave a slightly embarrassed shrug. "Oh, it wasn't that big a deal. It's all about knowing which vendors and which warehouses have the things you need. After that, it didn't take much time to pull it together."

Archie's classic, movie-star features were a study in amusement. "'Not much time' for Victoria meant being on the phone half the time and driving to Phoenix the other half. But I do have to admit this all looks very impressive."

That was for sure. Before I could respond, Josie came up to us, her round face all smiles, her plump form encased in a brilliant green sheath dress that, combined with her bright red hair, made her look like a walking advertisement for the holiday season.

"Isn't it wonderful?" she gushed, and then,

before any of us had a chance to respond, "But come along—I want to introduce you to our competitors."

Both Chuck and Hazel looked as though they would have preferred to grab a drink first, but since none of the waiters moving through the space with trays of champagne and glasses of beer was in our immediate vicinity, it looked as though my friends would have to forego their refreshments for the time being. Instead, Josie led us to an open space past the little brewers' rooms, where there were tables set up and a buffet of all sorts of delectable morsels placed off to one side.

Standing near that table was a tall man with sandy brown hair and sharp, attractive features. He appeared to be holding forth to a group of five or six people I didn't recognize, probably visitors who'd come from out of town to attend the competition.

"Ah, well," the man was saying in deprecating tones, "it's all a matter of degree, I suppose. I like to take the time to gather the perfect ingredients and make sure the conditions are exactly right before I start formulating a new brew, but I know some of the other brewers here are more interested in rushing things to market."

Everyone listening smiled, if a little awkwardly.

What an ass, I thought. However, I tried to arrange a pleasant expression on my face as Josie

went up to the stranger and said, "Trent, these are
some of my dearest friends here in Globe. This is
Calvin Standingbear, the chief of the San Ramon
tribal police, and his wife Selena Marx. She owns
Once in a Blue Moon, one of the shops downtown.
You've met Victoria Parrish, of course, and this is
her husband Archie, who has the dance studio
right next door to Selena's store. And this is Hazel
Marr, who runs the Airbnb that Sofia is staying in,
and Hazel's husband Chuck. He owns a ranch on
the west side of town. Everyone, this is Trent
Reynolds, one of our competitors."

Trent looked a little dazed at being hit with so
many different names at once, but his sandy
eyebrows pulled together as his gaze focused on me.
"Oh, you've got that woo-woo shop, right?"

Because I'd used that same term to describe my
store plenty of times, I wasn't at all offended by the
description. "Yes, it's a New Age store," I said
calmly. "And it's very nice to meet you, Trent. Josie
says you're thinking about possibly opening a
brewpub here in Globe."

Even as the words came out, I wondered if I
should have made the comment. Maybe Josie had
told me that particular tidbit in confidence and
didn't want to sound as though she was counting
her chickens before they hatched.

But Trent didn't look surprised or offended
that I'd been let it on the secret, and instead only

said, "I'm thinking about it. This area is ripe for development, and with those new houses going up east of town and more people wanting to get out of the Phoenix area and into someplace a little more livable, I think the time is right for a venture like mine to come in here and help revitalize your downtown."

Personally, I thought our downtown was just fine, what with my shop and Archie's studio and the various art galleries and coffee shops and restaurants. Heck, we even had a movie theater, even if it wasn't some huge twenty-screen multiplex.

"I like Globe just fine the way it is," Hazel remarked, her greenish eyes narrowed. Clearly, she didn't have much use for Trent Reynolds.

"It's a great place," Victoria, ever the peacemaker, said. "But that doesn't mean there isn't a little room for improvement."

Trent's gaze rested on her as she spoke, obviously admiring, and I felt rather than saw Archie bristle a bit. Before the moment could get too tense, though, Josie cut in, saying, "Well, we won't keep you, Trent. I want to introduce my friends to the rest of the brewers."

"Sure," Trent said, now looking utterly unconcerned. "I suppose that's the polite thing to do."

And then Josie bustled all of us off to meet the other competitors. The remaining contestants were four men and a single woman, something that surprised me a little, since I hadn't thought the balance of the sexes in the contest would be so lopsided. Then again, I thought I'd read somewhere that craft brewing was still very much a man's game, although more women were getting involved as time went on.

The next five minutes or so were a jumble of introductions and names. Sofia Barnes, the only woman in the group, was probably around my age, pretty in an off-hand kind of way, with blonde hair pulled into a messy knot at the back of her head and a scarf in muted shades of blue and brown holding the rest of her hair back from her face. I got the feeling she wore her hair that way when working and hadn't seen much reason to change it for the reception.

We were introduced to Elijah Wright and David Perry next, both of whom looked like they were probably in their late thirties. The latter was a good-looking guy with a hipster beard and man-bun, the latter causing Hazel to shoot a sly glance in my direction as Josie made the introductions. Elijah, who had a shaved head and intense dark eyes, appeared quiet and serious, and extremely uncomfortable with this sort of forced sociality, although he managed to mumble a "nice to meet you" when Josie brought us over to him.

The remaining two competitors, Matt Mitchell and Nick Russell, seemed pleasant enough, although their semi-scruffy appearance and general air of awkwardness told me they, too, would much rather have been in a kitchen somewhere stirring a malt than having to deal with a formal reception. When Josie got an idea into her head, however, there wasn't much point in trying to dissuade her.

Eventually, though, Josie left us to go talk to the Lewises, who'd just arrived. Henry also didn't seem thrilled to be here, and I had a feeling Joyce had told him he needed to put on his public face and go with the flow, since he was the one who'd agreed to be a judge in the first place.

They didn't make much of an effort to come over and chat with our little group, but that was fine. While the armed neutrality Henry and I had once shared had given way to a slightly more congenial rapport, it wasn't as though we were besties or anything close to it, and he probably thought it better to socialize with people in his and Joyce's own circle—local business owners, neighbors, other members of the Globe police department.

And now that we were past the awkward introductions, we were all able to get our own food and drink, and to indulge in a little gossip.

"That Trent guy seems like a real tool," Hazel said, and took a sip of champagne. "I'm not sure I even want him to have a brewpub here in Globe."

Chuck lifted an eyebrow and shot a quick glance in the direction of the object of her derision.

Luckily, Trent Reynolds appeared to be holding forth with yet another captive audience, so I doubted he'd heard anything of what she'd said.

"He does seem a little abrasive," Calvin commented, his tone neutral. In deference to my delicate condition, he was also sipping Perrier rather than helping himself to champagne or beer. "But if his brews are good, I suppose that doesn't matter. I kind of doubt he'd be involved with the day-to-day operation of the restaurant, even if he did open one here."

A girl could hope. I shared Hazel's assessment of the man in question, although I had to admit privately that it would be nice to have just a bit more variety in our town's culinary offerings. Cloud Coffee made impeccable sandwiches and pastries, but they weren't open for dinner. The Flatiron was a great place for lunch, although no one could accuse them of being fancy. And although Olamendi's was our go-to when we wanted to go out for dinner, I thought it would be nice to get a break from the burritos and the tacos every once in a while.

"And he complimented me on the designs I did for the competition and said he'd like to hire me to design the restaurant," Victoria put in. "I've only worked on houses so far, and that would be a fun challenge."

Archie appeared less than thrilled at the notion

of his beautiful wife being around Trent Reynolds during such a project, although he didn't say anything. My friend might have spent seventy-plus years in a cat's body, thanks to a dreadful curse a witch had cast on him back in the early 1950s, but he knew better than to tell Victoria what to do. She made her own choices concerning her business, and Archie seemed just fine with that.

"Well, if it'll bring more work your way, then I suppose it's a good thing," Hazel said. "And if the food's good, then I guess I can excuse Trent Reynolds for being a total jerk."

We all chuckled, and the conversation moved on to other subjects, including the big holiday party that Archie and Victoria would be throwing at their place on the twenty-third. Normally, I would have said that was putting a lot on her plate, since they'd just hosted their at-home wedding in mid-October.

But because Victoria had moved from wedding planning to interior design, I knew a gathering for fifty-odd people was child's play to her. Things had been busy enough that I hadn't had the chance to go over to her house and see all the holiday decorating she'd done, but I couldn't wait to attend the party, since I knew the place probably looked like something right out of a magazine...or someone's carefully curated Instagram feed.

By the time nine o'clock rolled around, we all

decided we'd put in enough face time, especially since Chuck always had to get up at the crack of dawn to check on his livestock. While I didn't need to be at the store until a little before ten, I was ready to call it a night as well. These days, even though my pregnancy was progressing with nary a hiccup and all seemed to be going well, I still got tired a lot faster than I had back in the days before I was incubating a tiny human inside me.

Calvin held my hand as we walked out to his Durango and helped me up into the passenger seat once we reached the SUV. Neither of us said anything as we pulled out of the parking lot and he pointed the vehicle east toward home.

But then he remarked, "Looks like Josie's got her hands full."

"Josie always has her hands full. She thrives on it," I replied, and my husband grinned, teeth glinting white in the reflected light from the dashboard.

"Fair enough," he said. "But still, she's having to corral a lot of personalities there. I could tell there wasn't much love lost between any of her competitors."

"Really?" I said. True, Trent Reynolds appeared to be the abrasive type who thought he was better than anyone else, but otherwise, I hadn't seen much interacting among the other competitors. "I don't think I even saw them talking to each other."

Calvin waited to turn onto Highway 70 before he answered.

"That's what I mean," he said. "If they were all friendly rivals, then they probably would have been chatting, talking about the competition. Instead, except for Matt Mitchell and Nick Russell, they looked as though they were doing their best to stay far out of each other's orbits."

Something that wasn't too difficult to do in a space the size of the converted gymnasium. But, even though the various brewers hadn't seemed overly friendly, I didn't think it was that big a deal. After all, they were there to compete against each other, not be best friends.

"Well, I'm sure Josie can handle it," I said. "I know they're all staying in different Airbnbs, so it's not as though they're going to be in each other's laps while they're here in town. They can all maintain their distance except for when the competition is actually happening."

"True," Calvin agreed.

It was time to turn onto the gravel lane that led to our house, so he didn't say anything for another moment, not until we'd pulled into the driveway and gotten out of the car. As he was unlocking the front door, he spoke again, his tone almost diffident.

"Did you see anything?" he asked.

I didn't bother to ask what he meant by "see." I stepped inside, then paused to pull off my wrap and hang it from the hall tree by the front door. "No, I didn't see any auras," I replied, guessing that was why he'd sounded just a little timid as he'd broached the subject. "But that's not too surprising. They always came and went of their own volition, and not because of anything I did." Smiling slightly, I added, "Not that I really needed my auras to pick up on the vibes in that room. Trent Reynolds seems like a serious blowhard, and the rest of them don't appear to have much use for him. The rest of it is just static."

Calvin came over and wrapped his arms around me, even as our little dog Sadie trotted toward us and demanded some attention after being left alone for several hours. We petted her and made much of her, and, satisfied, she headed off toward the bedroom and the little bed we kept for her there.

After placing a warm kiss on my cheek, my husband said, "I always did love your incisive commentary on human nature."

I arched an eyebrow at him. "Are you being sarcastic?"

"Not at all," he replied. "You've always been good at getting to the heart of the matter."

"Must be my Pluto in Scorpio," I joked, and he

hugged me a little tighter and kissed me again, a real kiss this time, warm and utterly welcome.

Hand in hand, we headed off to the bedroom, thinking only about each other, without any thoughts to spare for the High Country Brewing Competition.

THREE

We All Float

THE NEXT DAY DAWNED SUNNY AND bright. I kissed Calvin goodbye as he headed off for work and then took Sadie for a walk down the lane before it was my turn to gather my things and drive into town to get the workday started. Knowing Hazel would be at the shop today made me feel that much cheerier, since I figured we'd be able to chat about the brewers' reception the night before and share our opinions on the people we'd met. Victoria generally wasn't quite as much given to gossip—her years of working with Bridezillas had probably trained her to keep her lip zipped no matter how badly someone behaved—but there was always the possibility she'd drop in for a chat before she made her way to the upstairs studio that used to be my apartment.

Hazel wasn't the most punctual person in the

world, however, and that meant she didn't arrive until almost a quarter after the hour. Not a big deal...we rarely got busy until closer to lunchtime... and considering she was doing me a favor by coming in to help out on Fridays and Saturdays, I wasn't going to give her any grief over her late arrival.

"Sorry I'm late," she said breathlessly as she hurried in. "I forgot I had to stop for gas."

"It's not a problem," I assured her. "Not a single customer so far."

She slid her purse under the counter, placing it on the shelf next to mine. "I'd say that's good, but...."

"It's fine," I said. "Even when people are doing their holiday shopping, they're not beating down the door this early in the morning. Heard anything from Josie?"

"No," Hazel replied, now looking somewhat mystified. "Should I have?"

I shrugged, then reached for the refillable glass bottle of water I kept on the same shelf under the counter that we used to store our purses. Something about being pregnant made me feel thirsty all the time, although my doctor had assured me everything was fine and that it was good to stay hydrated.

"Well, you've got one of the brewers staying at your Airbnb," I said.

Hazel nodded, although I could tell she still couldn't figure out where I was going with this. "Yes, Sofia. It sounds like Josie fobbed all the guys off on Mavis, but the one female brewer is at my rental. Anyway, Sofia got here late yesterday afternoon and texted me to let me know she got into the house okay, but I haven't heard from her after we said hello at the reception last night. And I don't really expect to, unless something goes wrong with the heat or the plumbing or whatever."

"I doubt that's going to happen," I said with a smile. The house had been Hazel's before she moved in with Chuck, and I knew she'd done a lot of renovations when she first bought it some four years earlier. At any rate, the odds of the furnace croaking or the plumbing springing a leak seemed pretty low to me. "No," I went on, "I guess I just figured Josie might have wanted to check in with you and Mavis to see how all her competitors were doing."

"Josie was probably busy with closing down the reception last night," Hazel said. "And since she must have been out late, I doubt she was up early this morning."

Hazel's comment seemed like a logical enough assumption...except I knew Josie would never let a couple of hours of sleep get between her and whatever needed to be done that day. "Fair enough," I responded, since there didn't seem to be much point in arguing over such a nit-picky detail. "And I guess today should be pretty quiet, since she made it sound as if the competitors were going to be finishing prepping their stalls and getting ready for the contest tomorrow."

"That's the plan," Hazel agreed. "I know Sofia said she would be out early today because her business partner was driving down from Flagstaff with the stuff she bottled a couple of weeks ago, and she was going to meet him at the gym to get everything transferred and set up. It sounded like she wanted to keep it in her shop up north for as long as possible since it was bottled so recently."

That was a long drive. Luckily, the weather had been fairly clear, so I didn't think Sofia's partner would have too much trouble getting from northern Arizona all the way down to our little spot in the south-central part of the state. All the same, it wasn't a drive I'd care to take in mid-December, when you could still encounter patches of ice until you got well past Payson.

"Makes sense," I said.

Before I could add anything else, however, Josie burst into the shop, hands in the air, every inch of her rounded form shaking with worry.

"Calamity!" she cried out, and Hazel and I exchanged a surprised glance.

"What's a calamity?" I asked, although I had no

doubt Josie planned to tell us now that she had gotten past her startling announcement.

"Trent Reynolds," she said, something in her tone making it sound as though I should have known already, even though I'd patiently explained to her more than once that I wasn't a psychic. "Brett—he'd gone over to install a few more shelves in Trent's display space—found him floating in the vat in his room at the gym!"

Shock flooded through me, and, judging by Hazel's startled gasp, she was just as flabbergasted as I was. My friend found her voice first, though, asking, "How could Trent have been floating in one of those vats? I thought they were just for display."

"They were," Josie replied. She reached up to straighten the lapel of her black jacket, fingers pausing for a moment to touch the rhinestone Christmas tree pin there, as if doing so could reassure her there was still order in the universe somewhere. "But someone filled it up with water and dropped him in it."

This startling piece of information made Hazel and me trade another look. "Was there any sign of a struggle?" I said.

A nod. "Yes, Brett said a lot of the bottles on display in his 'room' got knocked over and were broken all over the floor. The medical examiner has

Trent's body now, and I suppose they're checking for signs of foul play."

It sure seemed to me there were plenty of signs already. Whatever had happened to Trent Reynolds after the reception was over and everyone else had gone home, it sounded as though he'd put up quite a fight.

"That's terrible," Hazel said, and she did look genuinely concerned, despite her comments about the brewmaster the evening before.

"Yes, it's awful," I chimed in, then paused before adding gently, "I'm sorry about your competition, Josie."

At once, she lifted her chin, pale blue eyes meeting mine. "Oh, I have no intention of calling it off. I want you to find Trent's killer, Selena. If you can find him before the judging starts, then everything can go ahead as planned."

For the second time in less than five minutes, I could only stare at Josie, feeling positively flummoxed. I managed to find my voice and said, "Um, Josie, the competition starts tomorrow. How in the world am I supposed to locate the killer that quickly?"

"I have supreme faith in you," she responded at once. "You've solved so many crimes, Selena. I know you can solve this one, too."

Obviously wanting to come to my aid, Hazel said, "Selena's great at tracking down murderers.

But she still needs some time to do it. Giving her only twenty-four hours is a big ask."

"It's a little more than twenty-four hours," Josie replied, clearly not dismayed by the impossible time frame involved. "The doors to the gym won't open until five tomorrow afternoon, and the judging doesn't start until six. That gives you more than thirty hours."

Oh, dear Goddess. While I'd always been happy to come to Josie's aid before—and while I knew how important this competition was to her—I didn't see how I could possibly bring someone to justice in less than a day and a half, especially since I didn't have any leads to go on.

"Isn't the gym an active crime scene right now?" Hazel inquired, and I wanted to hug her for bringing up such a practical complication.

Undaunted, Josie said, "It is, but Henry assured me that he and his deputies would be done with their work there sometime today. That means we're free to go back in Saturday morning, possibly even earlier."

There went that idea. However, just because the crime scene would be cleared in time for the competition didn't mean this still wasn't a terrible idea.

"Won't people think it's weird that we went ahead with the contest when a man was murdered there only two days earlier?" I said, to which Josie emphatically shook her head.

"Not at all," she replied. "I'm sure people will view it as forging ahead despite the tragedy. Besides, can you imagine the logistics of having to cancel all the food trucks and the security, of having to contact everyone who bought tickets and tell them the event has been canceled? They'll never trust the city of Globe to host an event ever again!"

Maybe that was being a little hyperbolic...or maybe not. After all, people did tend to get cranky when their plans were canceled at the last minute through no fault of their own. Even if they got their money refunded, they'd still probably have a hard time canceling their hotel rooms and would probably forfeit their deposits.

And I had to admit there was a certain sector of the population who would probably think that Trent Reynolds' murder added a little fillip to the occasion, gave it a bit of extra excitement. After all, it wasn't as if most of them would have known him, so there wasn't a lot of point in mourning a stranger.

I hated myself a little for entertaining such a notion, but I'd worked with people long enough to realize my unpleasant thoughts were nothing more than the sad truth.

So, as Hazel looked on with unbelieving eyes, I said slowly, "Okay, Josie. I'll see what I can do."

Obviously, there was no chance I'd be able to stay at the shop and conduct a murder investigation at the same time. After Josie left, telling us she needed to go talk to Henry, I turned toward Hazel. She shot me a lopsided smile.

"I know," she said. "You need to go play Sherlock Holmes. I can hold down the fort here."

"We can just close—" I began, but she cut me off.

"Not with a bunch of people coming into town for the brewing competition," she said. "You don't want to miss out on that business. I can handle it."

"Are you sure?" I asked. Yes, I appreciated her coming to my rescue, but I also didn't want to dump so much work on her with no backup.

"I'm sure," she replied. "It'll be fine." She paused there, hazel eyes glinting with curiosity. "What do you think you're going to do first?"

Kick myself in the head for agreeing to do something so crazy, I thought, but I only released a breath and said, "I need to consult the spiritual world for some guidance."

Sadie was thrilled to see me come home in the middle of the day, since I rarely drove to the house for lunch. The property Calvin and I shared was just far enough away from downtown that going back and forth would have taken up a big chunk of time, so I didn't really see the point.

Now, though, since I had absolutely nothing to go on when it came to tracking down Trent Reynolds' murderer, I needed to consult my Tarot cards and decide what to do next.

The little dog tagging at my heels, I headed into the secondary bedroom Calvin and I had turned into my office. Luckily, the house had four bedrooms, so we'd been able to convert the other spare room into a nursery without having to dislodge me from my office. However, if we decided in the future that we wanted our family to expand again, then we'd need to add on to the house. Some people might have suggested moving to a bigger place, but I loved the home that had been Calvin's first and was now both of ours, loved its warm, earthy Southwest charm and the beautiful, isolated spot where it was located. Because there was plenty of land, creating a five- or even six-bedroom house really wouldn't be a problem.

Better have this little one first and see how things go, I told myself, one hand moving over my rounded belly. Not for the first time, a little of shiver of mixed anticipation and fear passed over me. I was definitely looking forward to raising this child with Calvin...even as I couldn't quite keep myself from worrying about how awful the birth itself would be. We were taking Lamaze classes and doing all the right things, but still, I couldn't banish from my mind the image of me screaming at the top of my lungs for an epidural, stat, as I was wheeled into the delivery room.

But that day was still several months off in the future, while right now, I was staring down the barrel of an impossible deadline. I needed to concentrate on the task at hand and pray to all the goddesses and various powers of the universe that enough clues would fall into my lap to lead me to a quick solution.

All right, the universe didn't usually work that way, but a hedgewitch had to hope.

I got out my Everyday Witch tarot and went over to my altar. Although my nerves practically thrummed with the need to get this done quickly, I knew I couldn't rush. That was why I went ahead and lit a stick of white sage incense to clear the air, and why I also used my trusty Aim-n-Flame on several of the tea lights in their little stone candle-holders where they sat on my altar.

Just breathing in the incense and seeing the flickering flames of the candles made me feel a little better, a little calmer. Several more deep breaths as I shuffled the cards and did my best to focus on the task at hand.

Simply asking who had killed Trent Reynolds wouldn't give me the answers I needed. That wasn't how the Tarot operated. No, I had to try something else.

Why would someone want to murder Trent Reynolds?

I held that thought in my mind while I played with the cards. Then I felt the little tingle in my fingers that usually seemed to occur when the right card came to hand, so I drew it out of the deck and laid it down on my cheerful Yule altar cloth with its bright shades of red and green.

The King of Pentacles, reversed.

I didn't always do reversals in my readings, but in this case, the meaning was too clear to ignore. Trent Reynolds had crossed someone, it seemed, or someone was jealous of him and his success.

Jealousy was often a powerful motivator.

But had it been powerful enough to commit murder?

The next card was the Queen of Pentacles, also reversed, and I frowned. I knew I'd shuffled the cards carefully, so there was no physical reason why those two cards should have come in such close succession.

Again the theme of jealousy, although the inclusion of a card that almost always indicated a woman only made me frown a little more. Had a woman killed Trent Reynolds? Was there some sort of love triangle going on here?

My thoughts went immediately to Sofia Barnes, the only woman in the brewing competition. She definitely didn't seem like a murderer, had been quiet and soft-spoken when I met her at the reception. And, looking at the hard, cold facts and nothing else, she just didn't seem physically strong enough to wrestle someone like Trent Reynolds into a vat of water and hold his head down until he stopped breathing. If nothing else, he had to have been at least seven or eight inches taller than she and probably sixty or seventy pounds heavier.

But because the Queen of Pentacles reversed occupied such a strong position in this card pull, I realized I couldn't ignore Sofia, either. No, I'd have to weigh the merits of each of the competitors as a murderer, even though I knew the killer could have been someone who wasn't even participating in the brewing contest. Because it sounded as though Josie had worked very hard to get the word out over the past twenty-four hours, there were probably thousands of people who would have known exactly where Trent Reynolds would be on the evening of Thursday, December fourteenth.

I pushed that thought aside as best I could. The whole situation already felt overwhelming enough;

I didn't need to add in thousands more possible suspects.

The third card I drew was the Chariot, also reversed. In this case, I could only surmise that its presence in the reading meant I was dealing with some kind of quarrel or dispute, possibly even a lawsuit.

Had someone sued Trent Reynolds and then, when the case didn't go their way, decided to take him permanently out of the equation?

Well, I couldn't answer the second part of that question, but the first part shouldn't be too difficult.

I stepped away from my altar and went over to the easy chair in one corner, the spot where I'd dropped my purse as I came into the room. A quick rummage, and then my phone was in my hand.

Calvin picked up on the second ring. No hello, just, "I suppose you heard about what happened to Trent Reynolds."

News traveled fast in this part of the world. But then, I knew my husband had his informants in the Globe police department, although he would never tell me exactly who they were. It seemed some of Henry Lewis's own deputies thought I was better at solving crimes than their boss, so they funneled information to Calvin in order to get it to me.

"Josie told me how Brett found Trent's body,"

I said. Maybe I hesitated just a little, but then I realized my husband would find out about my silly promise eventually. "I told her I'd try to figure out who did it."

I couldn't see his smile, but somehow I was able to sense it anyway. "Why does that not surprise me?"

"I suppose it wouldn't," I admitted. "The twist here is that Josie wants me to get the whole thing figured out before the event begins on Saturday afternoon."

Now a warning note entered my husband's voice. "Selena—"

"I know, I know," I broke in. "It's kind of crazy. But I'm going to try my best, because I know how much this competition means to Josie. There's not going to be a brewpub now, I suppose, but it would still be better if we can show how quickly we were able to track down the killer. That would make people feel safer about attending the contest, don't you think?"

Calvin didn't answer right away, and for a second or two, I wondered if he was going to put his foot down and tell me a woman in my condition shouldn't be running around trying to track down a murderer. Not that Calvin was the type to issue ultimatums, but this wasn't just my safety involved, but the safety of our unborn child.

I held my breath, trying to figure out how to

tell him I was going to ignore his wishes. Luckily, I wasn't put up against that particular wall, because when he spoke again, he sounded resigned to the situation.

"I guess it would," he said. "And I have to assume you had a particular reason for calling me now."

Of course I did. He would suspect that, because we generally used texts to keep in touch during the workday, since they were so much less intrusive than a phone call.

"Yes," I said. "Can you have Ben check to see if Trent Reynolds was involved in any lawsuits? I'm trying to establish a motive."

Ben Ironhorse was one of Calvin's deputies, a twenty-four-year-old whiz kid who seemed able to hack just about anything that needed hacking. In this case, though, I guessed he wouldn't have to do anything illegal, but simply perform a couple of quick database searches to see if anyone was in the process of suing Trent Reynolds. I probably could have done much the same thing, except it would have taken me three times as long.

"Sure, Ben's on duty today," Calvin said. Since I wasn't anywhere close to being in a gray area with my request, he obviously didn't see the need to tell me this was something I shouldn't be doing. "He can probably have an answer for you in the next half hour."

Even better. While my hopes of getting all this resolved before Saturday evening weren't very high, it still made me feel better to know this search wouldn't take too much time. If I were lucky, I'd get the kind of actionable information that might help me get that much closer to discovering who had hated Trent Reynolds so much they'd decided to drown him in a place where he was sure to be easily discovered.

"Great," I said. "I'm going to be at the house for a while, trying to work my way through this, so I'll wait here for your call."

"Sounds good." Calvin paused there for a moment, as though weighing his next words before he spoke them. "Selena...you need to be careful."

"I *am* being careful," I told him. "Right now, I'm at home, and I'm going to try researching the other brewers from here. Nothing's going to happen."

"Nothing until you step outside the house," he said wryly.

Okay, he had me there. And I definitely wasn't going to point out to him that our house wasn't quite the sanctuary he thought it was, not when murderous Mark Lemmon had tried to assault me right here in our kitchen. Luckily, my quick thinking with the Instant Pot had saved the day, but still, using small kitchen appliances in self-defense wasn't the sort of experience I wanted to repeat any time soon.

"Well, I'm staying put for at least a little bit," I replied. "And after that...yes, I'll be careful. I'll make sure to text you where I'm going and when, and I'll let you know when I plan to check in so you can tell if too much time has gone by since my last message."

This must have all sounded eminently reasonable to my husband, because he didn't bother to argue with me. "It's a plan," he said. "And I'll call you again as soon as Ben has any information for me."

"Love you," I said simply.

"Love you more."

Smiling to myself, I ended the call and went over to my desk so I could fire up my laptop. The phone sat only a few inches away from my mouse pad, guaranteeing that I'd be able to grab it on the first ring.

Until then, though...

...until then, I had some research to do.

FOUR

The Usual Suspects

CORRECTION—I HAD A *LOT* OF RESEARCH to do. Even though Josie had whittled her desired ten brewing competitors down to only six...and even though one of those brewers was now in the morgue...trying to poke and prod at the motivations of five different people seemed like a heck of a lot of work.

Well, time to start with the basics.

I decided to leave Sofia Barnes for last, just because I still couldn't believe someone her size could have possibly possessed the strength to wrestle Trent Reynolds into submission and into the gleaming copper vat that had been part of the set decoration of his competition space. Instead, I figured I might as well start looking into the brewers in the order I'd met them at the reception the night before, which meant the first subject of my investigation was Elijah Wright.

At first glance, I didn't see anything too noteworthy about his background. Thirty-nine years old, he'd gone to New Mexico State University in the southern New Mexico town of Las Cruces, and had worked at a couple of local breweries before deciding to strike out on his own. He'd won several ribbons at the New Mexico State Fair and at brewing competitions around the Southwest, and currently was in the process of opening his own brewpub in a small town called Anthony, located about a half hour south of Las Cruces and right on the border with Texas.

But then I found a snippet on someone's blog talking about the way Elijah and Trent had gotten in each other's faces at a brewing contest in a place called Ruidoso, a confrontation that had supposedly occurred because Trent had accused Elijah of stealing his India pale ale recipe. The two hadn't exactly come to blows, but it definitely sounded as if security had had to step in to separate the pair.

Interesting. I certainly couldn't claim to know much about Elijah Wright as a person, except that my initial impression of him had been one of a quiet, intense man, the sort of guy who would much rather have stayed out of the spotlight. He didn't seem the type to engage in casual brawling, making me believe he'd most likely only been defending himself when Trent flew off the handle.

Then again, someone that quiet and reserved probably didn't share much of what they were thinking. Was Elijah the kind of man who would brood in silence, who would plot and plan and wait for the perfect opportunity to present itself so he could enact his revenge?

Maybe. Still, even though I didn't have any real answers, at least I knew there had definitely been some bad blood between him and Trent.

From what I could tell from my online research, David Perry appeared to be Elijah's polar opposite. All the coverage I found seemed to reveal a man who was all too aware of his good looks and made sure to leverage them to earn himself as much publicity as possible. He hailed from Cottonwood, Arizona, and was a partner in a brewery located there. Not as many medals as Elijah Wright, but David Perry's beers and ales had earned him a silver and a bronze at the Arizona State Fair, which seemed to be all the bona fides he'd needed to start his business.

Someone who appeared to have such a need for attention didn't seem like the type to skulk in the shadows and throttle his rival, but I'd be the first person to admit that people's public and private faces could be very different.

Also, there was that man-bun.

I shook my head at myself, since I knew I was being way too judge-y on that point, and moved on to the last two competitors, Matt Mitchell and Nick Russell. When I'd met them the night before, neither one of them had made much of an impression. They'd both seemed like people who preferred to let their work speak for itself, and in appearance, they hadn't been terribly different from one another, either, both of them in their late thirties or early forties, wearing Henley-style long-sleeved T-shirts that were probably their version of formal wear, along with jeans they deemed suitable for dress-up because they didn't have any noticeable holes or stains.

However, a little poking around told me they were two very different people. Matt Mitchell had a master's in chemistry and had basically upended his life only about four years earlier, when he'd ditched a cushy job at a pharmaceutical company and taken a hard left into the wild world of craft brewing. Nick Russell, on the other hand, seemed like a party guy who'd bounced from job to job until he ended up working at a brewery in Flagstaff and realized he had a knack for that sort of thing.

All of this was information I could put in my back pocket against further need, but at the moment, none of it seemed to provide any clues as to why one of these people might have wanted Trent Reynolds dead.

Okay, time to look into Sofia Barnes.

At just thirty, she was definitely the youngest of the group of competitors. She'd attended NAU in Flagstaff, had gotten a degree in biochemistry, and had worked in the food service industry for several years before ending up taking some brewing courses and deciding she'd found her calling. The local newspaper had published a piece on her only a few months ago, talking about the new brewpub she and her business partner, a man named Kurt Vonn, were planning to open in Flagstaff's historic downtown.

She seemed to be doing very well for herself, so I didn't see any real reason for her to have been jealous of Trent Reynolds. Then again, even though my gut was telling me that my interpretation of the card reading I'd performed a while earlier was correct, I didn't know that for sure. Right now, I was just going on instinct.

And even though I still didn't think she was guilty, she seemed like the easiest person for me to approach. Because she was staying in Hazel's Airbnb, I could reach out to my friend and see if she could arrange a meeting. Trying to talk to the other four competitors might be a little trickier, so I figured it couldn't hurt to start with the path of least resistance and then go from there.

I reached for my phone and entered the number for the store—that and Calvin's cell were about the only ones I had memorized—and waited for Hazel to pick up.

"Hi, you've reached Once in a Blue Moon. How can I help you?"

"Hi, Hazel," I said. "How's everything going?"

"Fine," she replied. "We've had a few customers so far. What's up?"

"Can you get in touch with Sofia Barnes and see if I can go talk to her sometime this morning?"

"Sure," my friend said right away. "Following a lead?"

I wished. "Not really," I said. "Right now, I'm just trying to get more information from each of the brewers. I figure I need to meet with them one on one if possible, since I really don't know much about any of them."

"And meeting them for a minute at a reception wasn't the best way to pick up on their vibes," Hazel remarked. I couldn't see her, but I had a feeling she was smiling a little. "I get it. Hang on a sec—I'll text her."

A small clunk that was probably Hazel setting the shop phone down on the countertop—I used a wireless model, but it was still a landline—followed by a few click-y noises that were probably her firing off a quick text to Sofia. A moment later, Hazel picked up again.

"Okay, you're set," she said. "I told Sofia that you're someone who solves a lot of crimes here in town and that you're trying to get to the bottom of what really happened to Trent Reynolds."

At this piece of unwelcome information, I tried not to wince. I loved Hazel and would have done anything for her, but she wasn't exactly the most discreet person in the world. Now that Sofia Barnes knew I was investigating Trent Reynolds' death, there was pretty much zero chance I'd get her to let anything slip if it turned out she was the actual killer.

Well, done was done. I had other ways of gathering information that had nothing to do with directly interviewing a person.

If, of course, my auras decided to cooperate.

I thanked Hazel for her help, told her to let Sofia know I'd be over in about fifteen minutes, and then set down the phone. Because I'd already gone to the shop this morning, thinking I was going to work a full day, I was dressed and had my hair and makeup done, so I wouldn't have to waste any time on that.

But since I didn't know how long I was going to be gone—this could be a quick there-and-back trip, or I could pick up another lead that required me to be away from the house for an extended period—I went ahead and took Sadie for a short walk up and down the lane, just so she could get her wiggles out and take care of business. We had a dog door, but when it was cold like this, she wasn't too motivated to go in and out unless she had absolutely no other alternatives.

With that task handled—and after I fired off a quick text to Calvin, letting him know I was going to talk to Sofia—I went to the garage and got in my Renegade, then headed toward the highway, driving west into town. I knew exactly where Hazel's Airbnb was located, since I'd spent plenty of time with her there before she moved in with Chuck. It was a cute little yellow-painted cottage, with a yard that was lush in the spring and summer but looked a little sparse at this time of year, with none of the flowers blooming and no snow to cover the frost-dried grass.

In a funny twist of fate, it turned out the house had also once belonged to Archie when he lived here in the 1950s before he was turned into a cat. He was declared missing at some point afterward, and the cottage sold and then sold again, eventually ending up in Hazel's hands. I'd actually offered to buy it from Hazel and give it back to him, but he'd declined, telling me it didn't really feel like home anymore. Just as well, because then he met Victoria, and they ended up buying a much larger house in a different part of town.

Still, it always felt a little strange to come here when I knew the place was occupied by one of Hazel's guests. She'd been going back and forth over whether she should just sell the house and be done with it, since it wasn't bringing in as much income as she'd thought it would, but it sounded like in this case, Josie had made her an offer she couldn't refuse in terms of putting up one of the brewing contest's competitors at the place.

Sofia answered the door almost as soon as I knocked, telling me she clearly had been waiting for me to arrive. As far as I could see, there weren't any obvious signs of grief in her face, nothing to tell me that Trent's passing had been anything more than an unexpected bump in the road.

"Come on in," she said, and moved out of the way so I could come inside. The main room hadn't changed materially since Hazel had converted the cottage to an Airbnb, had the same cheerful color scheme of yellow and blue and green, although she'd removed some of her own paintings that she'd had hanging there and replaced them with much less valuable prints.

"Thank you for seeing me," I replied, and Sofia only tilted her head slightly, interest clear in her bright green eyes.

"Well, I'll admit I was curious about talking to a real-life private detective."

I shook my head at that description. "Oh, I'm not a private eye. Solving crimes has turned into sort of a hobby for me. In this case, I'm trying to help Josie so she can salvage the competition."

Sofia had gone ahead and sat down in the wing

chair by the couch, obviously inviting me to take a seat on the sofa. I lowered myself to the cushion, even as the other woman looked at me in some puzzlement.

"Couldn't the competition go ahead anyway?" she asked. "I know that sounds callous, but if the police have cleared the scene by the time the event starts, I really don't see why you have to solve the murder before then."

She had a point, one I privately agreed with. "I suppose from a legal standpoint, that's true," I said. "But Josie would really like to have this wrapped up before then, if only to assure people it's perfectly safe to attend and that there's not some crazed killer lurking around the venue."

Now Sofia's lips curved in a small smile. The expression lit up her face, making her seem much prettier and more approachable than the awkward woman I'd met the night before. "This didn't seem like a random act of violence to me, though. It feels...personal."

"Did Trent have a lot of enemies?" I asked, frankly curious.

Her smile broadened. "I guess it depends on how you define 'enemies.' He's definitely pissed off a lot of people along the way, just because he's pretty arrogant and thinks he's head and shoulders above the rest of us peons who're working in the industry. Whether he got someone angry enough for them to want to kill him is an entirely different question, though. Mostly, it's all been a lot of trash talk."

"What about that incident with Elijah Wright at the brewing competition in Ruidoso?"

At once, Sofia's expression sobered. "Well, I wasn't there, so I don't know exactly what happened."

Damn. I'd really been hoping she might have attended the event so she would have observed the altercation in person.

"But," she went on before I could comment, "I heard about it through the grapevine. As usual, Trent was talking his regular smack, and Elijah just couldn't take it anymore. I don't think anyone really blames him for taking a swing at Trent."

"Do you think Elijah wanted Trent out of the way?" I inquired. He seemed like the most likely subject to me, but a lot of the time, that didn't mean much.

She shook her head. "No. I mean, they really disliked each other, but I think Elijah would rather have had Trent around so he could beat him by proving he makes better beer. Humiliating Trent Reynolds would have been much more his speed."

Interesting. So, there was definitely no love lost between the two men, but it sounded to me as though Elijah had a vested interest in making sure Trent was alive and breathing, not drowned in a vat that shouldn't have contained any water in it at all.

Which made me wonder who had filled the thing in the first place. The old gymnasium still had a functioning kitchen attached, so there was definitely water available, but it would have taken hours to fill one of those vats even using gallon jugs to transport the water.

Maybe someone had attached a hose to the faucet. I'd never done such a thing, but I had to believe it was possible. If that was what had happened, then the killing had definitely been premeditated by someone who'd known Trent would be at the reception site after everyone else had gone home that night.

"Do you know why Trent stayed at the gym after the reception was over?" I asked then, and Sofia shrugged.

"I heard him saying something to Josie Woodward about wanting to rearrange some of the stuff in his display space, but she made it sound as if she didn't have an extra key to the facility and that he'd just have to come in sometime today to take care of it." Sofia stopped there, a somewhat sad expression now flitting across her delicate features. "But obviously, that's not what happened."

No, it wasn't. Trent had either remained behind against Josie's wishes, or she'd given in and allowed him to stay on site. Either way, I guessed that I needed to talk to her next after I finished this interview with Sofia.

"Did anyone else know he wanted to stay behind?" I said, knowing I was probably reaching but unsure as to what other line of inquiry I should follow.

Another small head shake. "I don't think so. The only reason I heard him ask in the first place was because I was walking past them to get some more food from the buffet."

So much for that line of questioning. Anyone who hadn't met her would have said overhearing Trent's request provided even more of a reason to believe in Sofia Barnes' guilt, but I wasn't buying it. Not after talking to her and seeing up close how small and fragile she appeared. There was no way in the world someone her size could manhandle the six-foot-plus Trent Reynolds and hold him down while he drowned in a huge copper vat.

And even as that thought was passing through my head, Sofia's aura flickered into view. Only for a second, just long enough for me to see that it was a soft, soft blue touched with little flickers of deep rosy pink. I guessed those darker shades indicated her worry about the current situation, but there was absolutely nothing in them to indicate she was feeling guilty about anything.

True, that sort of evidence wasn't exactly admissible in a court of law. All the same, it told me

I was going to have to look elsewhere to discover who'd actually killed Trent.

"I wish I could tell you more," she went on. "But I just don't know much about what happened. I came back here around a little before ten and talked to Kurt—he's my business partner —to firm up our plans for bringing down my latest batch of Bellemont Blonde for the competition. And after that I went to bed."

Something that could be proven by checking her phone records, but I wasn't going to make that kind of intrusive request. Maybe Henry would, if he even bothered to talk to her at all. I had a much better track record than the police chief for this kind of thing, and yet I guessed he would have already come to the same conclusion that I had— that Sofia Barnes was as innocent as the rest of us.

"Well, thank you for talking to me," I said. "I won't take up any more of your time."

With those words, I rose from the couch, and Sofia got up from her chair as well. Her expression was still a little worried as she walked me to the door.

"I hope you catch whoever did this," she said.

"So do I," I replied, and made my way down the porch steps.

Whether or not I'd be able to accomplish such a feat before tomorrow afternoon was an entirely separate problem.

FIVE

Key Questions

AFTER I DROVE AWAY FROM THE AIRBNB, I headed toward Josie Woodrow's real estate office downtown. There was always the chance she would be in her other office, the one at City Hall she used when carrying out her mayoral duties, but I doubted it. As far as I was able to tell, she spent much more time selling and showing houses than she did running Globe. Which made sense—our small town had been putting along just fine for the last hundred-plus years, so it didn't need a lot of micro-management.

Sure enough, Josie was sitting in her pink-painted real estate office when I stuck my head inside.

"Any leads?" she inquired at once, and I tried not to wince.

Way too many people had been asking me that same question lately.

"Not really," I said as I came in. She pointed toward the cream-upholstered chair in front of her desk, and I sank down in it. "Or at least, right now I'm mostly just collecting information. I went and talked to Sofia Barnes, and she told me how Trent Reynolds had wanted to stay at the site after the reception and you told him that wasn't possible."

Josie's lips pressed together. Today she was wearing scarlet lipstick to go with her bright jacket, and, combined with her hair, she was a study in shocking red.

"He did ask me, and I had to say no."

"Because you only had one key?"

Now she looked almost indulgent. "No, there's more than one key. I have a copy, and the other one is in the facilities manager's office at City Hall. But I still wasn't going to give one to Trent."

"Because you didn't trust him?" I asked, and her eyes narrowed slightly.

"That's a harsh way of putting it," she said. "Let's just say I didn't think it was a good idea to allow any of the competitors to be there unsupervised, not when most of them except Sofia already had at least some of their beer on display. I didn't want to run the risk of anything being tampered with."

That sure sounded like a lack of trust to me,

although I didn't press the issue. Instead, I clasped my hands in my lap, saying, "Do you know if Chief Lewis found any signs of forced entry?"

"No," she replied. "That's part of the puzzle. None of the doors to the gymnasium—or to the rest of the old high school—seemed to have been tampered with at all. So Henry really doesn't know how the killer got in."

Maybe they'd picked the locks, although I remembered that Calvin had told me once you could usually find some evidence to show a lock had been tampered with if you knew what to look for.

"Do you have your key?" I asked next.

At once, she opened her desk drawer and pulled out an oversized forest green purse decorated with studs and rhinestones. A few seconds of rummaging, and then she lifted up an equally oversized keychain with various penlights and metal charms and other odds and ends hanging from it. There had to have been at least fifteen keys attached to the ring, so it took her a moment or two to go through all of them.

"Yes, it's here," she said, separating out a big, official-looking brass key with "Do Not Duplicate" stamped on it. "And it was in my bag all night and came home with me, so I don't see how anyone could have used it."

"You didn't have your purse with you when I

saw you at the reception, though," I pointed out. "Where was it?"

Now looking a little perturbed, she replied, "Well, my bag was too big and heavy to lug around all evening, so I left it with Courtney Hill, the girl who was taking coats at the door."

Pretty blonde Courtney seemed like the last person to be in cahoots with a murderer. On the other hand, I supposed it was possible she'd been distracted by something or other, and the killer had taken advantage of her distraction to extract the key without her noticing.

But Josie had said she'd taken the bag home with her, which meant the killer couldn't have kept the key all night. Had he pocketed it, slipped away, and had it duplicated someplace where no one apparently paid any attention to the admonishment engraved on the key that it shouldn't be copied?

I supposed that scenario was possible...barely. Or....

"What about the key in the facilities administrator's office?" I asked.

Josie's penciled auburn brows drew together. "I think it's very unlikely that anyone could have taken that one. Cliff—the facilities director—is the only person with a key to his office except the custodial staff."

Custodians who came in after-hours to clean. One of them could have easily taken the key without anyone noticing.

Of course, that theory circled back to the obvious reality that they wouldn't have had any reason to take it. I didn't know the custodians who took care of City Hall, but since those were decent-paying government jobs with full benefits, I kind of doubted they'd put such a position in jeopardy just to steal a key for a sketchy brewer from Phoenix.

But since I knew I wasn't in a position where I could leave a single stone unturned, I told Josie, "Well, let's go talk to Cliff about the key. Maybe this is just a wild goose chase, but I don't want to ignore something that might be crucial to solving the case."

She glanced down at her watch, which, of course, boasted a cheerful green strap with bright red holly berries embroidered on it. "All right. He shouldn't have left for lunch yet."

We were cutting it close—we had about ten minutes until noon—but luckily, City Hall was only a five-minute walk away.

That was why Josie hoisted her purse over one shoulder, locked up her office, and gamely headed over to the imposing building just a block from my store. Once upon a time, the steep front steps wouldn't have posed any problems for me, but I was feeling a little winded by the time we reached the large double doors that allowed entry to the main floor.

Maybe I needed to add an extra fifteen minutes to my morning workout on the treadmill in my office...or maybe I just needed to realize that my six-months-pregnant body couldn't do everything my pre-pregnancy body could.

I followed along as Josie led me down the wide hallway that bisected the building, then over to an ancient elevator. As the doors groaned shut, she said, "I figured you probably didn't want to climb any more stairs."

No, I didn't...although I wasn't sure how much trust I could place in the creaking elevator that slowly made its way up to the second floor.

However, it got us to our destination without incident, and we stepped into a corridor not quite as wide as the one we'd left behind. The facilities director's office was only a few doors down—a door that opened just as we approached.

"Josie," said the man who'd begun to step into the hallway. He looked like he was in his late fifties, with balding light brown hair and glasses. "I didn't know you planned to stop by."

"Oh, I just needed to check on something," she replied in her usual airy tones, as though our current mission had nothing to do with the murder mystery I was trying to solve. "Cliff, this is my friend Selena Marx. Selena, this is Cliff Ivins, our facilities director."

He extended a hand at once and I shook it, feeling vaguely absurd. Handshakes had always seemed like an odd and archaic custom to me.

With that business out of the way, Josie went on, "I just wanted to check the keys for the gym in case I need to give the spare set to one of the people working security."

Cliff gave her a startled look. "You're still going to hold the competition? I thought—"

"Well, the disclaimer on the tickets said the event would go on, rain or shine," she cut in, still in the too-bright tone I knew she tended to employ whenever she was doing her best to ignore an unpleasant reality. "And I suppose that includes murder. Anyway, Henry told me his deputies would be done with the site sometime today, so it's not as if we can't go in there. It will be fine."

The expression Cliff wore told me he thought it would be anything but fine. However, it seemed he knew Josie just as well as I did—maybe better, since they'd probably been acquainted much longer than she and I had—because he didn't argue with her and only said, "Sure. Let me go get them."

He went back into his office, while Josie and I waited in the hall. I'd been halfway expecting him to return immediately, exclaiming that the keys were missing, but instead he came back with a set of two keys dangling from a woven leather lanyard, the kind of thing someone's kids might make at summer camp or something. For all I knew, that's exactly where he'd gotten it.

"Here you go," he said. "I guess it's good you're going ahead with the competition. I'm sure lots of people would be disappointed if you had to cancel it."

"That was exactly my thought," Josie replied. If she was at all fazed by the keys being exactly where they were supposed to be and not stolen by the murderer so he could whack Trent Reynolds with impunity, her expression showed no sign of it. No, she just took the spare set from him and slipped it into her purse. "Thanks, Cliff. We'll let you get on with your lunch."

"Not a problem," he responded at once.

Because he was also heading out of the building, the three of us shared a somewhat uncomfortable elevator ride down to the ground floor. Josie and I couldn't really discuss the surprising presence of the keys in Cliff's office, since doing so would only tip him off that we'd expected them to have been stolen.

After we'd said goodbye and begun to make our way back toward Josie's office, I waited until Cliff was safely traveling in the opposite direction

—probably to get a sandwich and a drink from Cloud Coffee—before saying, "Now what?"

Being Josie, she didn't look overly perturbed. "Now I suppose we need to wait for Courtney to get out of class so we can talk to her."

The local high school wouldn't let out for three hours. Considering the time frame I had to work with, sitting around and waiting until we could ask Courtney whether she'd noticed anything suspicious the night before probably wasn't a very good idea.

Before I could think of a tactful way to say I didn't have that much time to waste, my phone pinged from inside my purse. Murmuring an apology to Josie, I pulled it out and took a quick glance at the home screen.

Jackpot—a text from Calvin, with just the kind of information I'd been hoping for.

Elijah Wright is involved with litigation accusing Trent Reynolds of stealing the formula for his Chile Whisperer IPA. They were supposed to appear in court next week.

Okay, maybe not the jackpot I'd been hoping for. Yes, Calvin's deputy had learned that Elijah and Trent were wrangling legally, but if the case was about to be heard by a judge, why jump the gun and kill Trent so close to the time when Elijah might get some satisfaction from the courts?

"What is it?" Josie asked.

"Calvin found out that Elijah was suing Trent over a supposedly stolen beer formula," I replied.

"Well, then," she said, sounding triumphant and relieved at the same time. "That certainly gives Elijah Wright a motive for killing Trent."

"Maybe, maybe not," I told her. "You'd think Elijah would have rather had vindication from a judge and maybe some kind of restitution rather than drowning his rival in a brewer's vat."

The sunny expression Josie had been wearing immediately vanished. "Oh, I suppose you have a point there."

"But it's hard to say," I added. "I think what I really need to do now is go talk to Elijah Wright."

Josie was able to supply me with the addresses of the various Airbnbs where the competitors were staying, and also provided the useful tidbit that Henry Lewis had told them all to stay in town. Not that I'd really been expecting any of them to fly the coop, not when the contest was apparently going forward as planned, but still, I thought my chances of catching Elijah at his vacation rental were probably pretty good.

However, I really wasn't looking forward to the encounter. Sure, by this point I had plenty of experience trying to winnow information out of often reluctant suspects, but all the same, something about Elijah Wright intimidated me. I supposed part of it could be that he reminded me uncomfortably of Lucien Dumond, the former head of the Greater Los Angeles Necromancers' Guild...and the man whose unhealthy interest in me had led me to flee to Globe in the first place.

Elijah wasn't a necromancer, of course, but he was tall and bald and had piercing dark eyes. He might not have been able to stand in for Lucien himself, but he definitely could have played him in a TV movie of his life.

However, I didn't have time to dither and be nervous. No, I had to march right up to the door of Elijah's Airbnb, knock, and hope he was home.

Which was exactly what I did, even though I noted, with an extra twinge of nerves, that this was the same vacation rental where reality TV host Dillon James had once stayed and where he'd been killed by his producer while lying in a drunken stupor on one of the chaise lounges in the backyard.

Had Josie's friend Mavis informed Elijah that someone had died on the property?

I didn't know for sure. Arizona law required you to divulge that there had been a death in a house when you were selling it, but I had no idea whether the same rules applied to vacation rentals.

Even if he knew, I doubted that Elijah Wright

would have been put off by the news. He didn't seem like the type of person to rattle easily, altercations at brewfests in Ruidoso notwithstanding.

I lifted my hand and knocked on the door. A moment later, Elijah opened it, his heavy dark brows pulling together in confusion as he spied me on the doorstep.

"Um...Selena Marx, right?" he said, after apparently dredging up that bit of information from somewhere in the depths of his brain.

"Right," I said. Should I be glad that he'd remembered me?

Then again, he probably hadn't met too many pregnant brunettes at the reception last night.

Before I could dwell on that question for too long, I went on, "Do you mind if I talk to you for a minute?"

Now looking slightly startled, he said, "I guess not. Come on in."

I followed him inside, even as I wondered how he'd managed to snag this particular Airbnb, which was definitely the biggest and nicest of the vacation rentals Mavis owned. Maybe she'd picked the names out of a hat or something, because otherwise, I was sure Trent Reynolds would have done his darnedest to claim this spot as his home base while he was staying in town.

Elijah led me into the living room, a tastefully

furnished space with a vaulted ceiling overhead and a large plaster fireplace at one end. The hearth was cold and dark at the moment, however, since the sunny day didn't really require the assistance of a warm fire, even though the temperatures today would have to struggle to get out of the fifties.

"Want a seat?" Elijah asked, even as he bent down to pick up the remote for the TV mounted over the fireplace so he could turn off the football game currently playing there.

"Thanks," I said as I sat down on the ivory linen couch. The upholstery wouldn't have been my first choice for a vacation rental, but it seemed to be holding up fine so far. Maybe Mavis had someone come in and clean the furniture on a regular basis. "I was hoping I could talk to you about Trent Reynolds."

At once, Elijah's face—not the most expressive at the best of times, as far as I was able to tell—seemed to shut down. "I already told the police everything I know."

"I'm not the police," I assured him. "I'm just trying to help Josie Woodrow get to the bottom of Trent's death."

On my drive over to the house, I'd decided to be honest about my role in all this, since Hazel had already let the cat out of the bag about my being involved with the murder investigation, and it certainly wouldn't have done me any good to hand one story to one person participating in the brewing competition and something entirely different to another. I didn't know for sure how much they talked to one another...if at all...but it wasn't a risk I wanted to take.

To my surprise, Elijah seemed almost heartened by that bit of information, as if he was glad someone other than the local police was involved in trying to figure out what exactly had happened to Trent Reynolds the night before. In fact, Elijah's aura shimmered into existence for a second or two before disappearing again, telling me that, even though he might physically resemble Lucien Dumond a little more than I would have liked, in personality they were not the same at all.

The aura I'd seen so briefly was a deep, deep blue shading into violet, calm and serene, with none of the little accent colors I sometimes saw in other people's auras when they were dealing with conflicting emotions. In fact, the color violet was associated with the crown chakra, denoting spiritual maturity and a connection with the higher planes.

It didn't seem like the sort of aura I'd associate with someone who'd tried to throttle Trent Reynolds in public, but then, people could be very complicated.

Elijah wrapped his hands around one jean-clad

knee and surveyed me for a moment. Today he was wearing a dark blue fleece hoodie and lace-up boots, and looked as though he was ready to go hiking rather than hang around the house. Then again, he'd probably started his day thinking he was going to head over to the site of the brewing competition and work on his display, but, like the rest of the contestants, he couldn't go near the place until the police had given the all-clear.

"Well, I don't think it's any secret that I couldn't stand the guy," Elijah said. He had a deep voice, calm and almost contemplative. It would have been perfect for making recordings of guided meditations. However, his current subject matter was anything but soothing. "In fact, I was supposed to be in court next week to deal with a lawsuit about the formula he stole from me."

"You know for a fact that he did steal it?" I asked. What I knew about brewing could probably fit in my shoe, so I had no idea how easy it was to tell if a particular beer had been copied from someone else's recipe.

Elijah released an annoyed breath. "Yeah, I did. I came up with that brew. It was supposed to be my entry at the competition in Ruidoso last spring."

"Which was when you decked him," I said, figuring there wasn't any point in beating around the bush on that particular topic.

Now looking a little rueful, Elijah reached up

to rub his shaved head. "Well, I didn't have a chance to really get a punch in, because security pulled me back before I could do any damage. But yeah, I tried. He deserved it, the asshole."

Since I wasn't exactly a fan of Trent Reynolds, I couldn't argue with Elijah's comment. Not that I believed physical violence was ever the solution, but just because I knew how it felt to have your last nerve plucked to distraction.

"So, you decided to sue him instead of punch him," I observed, trying not to smile.

"Doing your homework, huh?"

I shrugged, even as I wished he'd offered me some water. My throat was starting to feel a little dry.

However, since I could tell Elijah wasn't really thinking about his duties as a host, I decided to forge ahead. "I try to learn what I can," I said, deciding it was probably better not to mention that my husband was the chief of the local tribal police and that I had more resources at my fingertips than most people. Curious, I asked, "Do you think the judge would have ruled in your favor?"

"Probably," Elijah replied without even a second of hesitation. "I had an independent lab analyze Reynolds' IPA and mine, and they came back nearly identical. Because I always document my work when I'm creating a new brew, I had plenty of notes and failed versions to prove I came up with the formula months before he supposedly did."

Although I was certainly not an expert, it did sound to me as though he had his bases covered. "What was Trent's response to the lawsuit?"

Elijah made a disgusted sound. "He wanted to settle out of court. I think he knew I had the goods on him, and he just wanted to make the whole thing go away. But I wasn't interested in that—I wanted to prove in court that he was a liar and a thief, and that he'd only gotten where he was from buying other people's formulas when he could and stealing them when he couldn't."

This comment served to reinforce my earlier belief that it didn't make any sense for Elijah to kill Trent now when he was so close to having his day in court. No, it sounded as if he'd had a much different kind of revenge in mind.

"If he was such a crappy beer-maker, why was he so popular?" I asked then.

This question didn't exactly earn me an eye roll, but Elijah's expression was close. "Because his family has a ton of money, and he used that to leverage his way into the craft brew community. I don't know why he didn't just go fly a private plane or whatever else rich people do to amuse themselves, but I know he bought out a small brewery, supposedly 'improved' their formulas, and started crafting a persona for himself. In reality, though, the guy was a total fraud."

Well, that story definitely explained why he'd felt the need to steal Elijah's formula. Some people couldn't be bought, but Trent had refused to allow that particular roadblock to stand in his way.

And now he was dead. While I didn't think Elijah Wright had anything to do with his rival's death, the information he'd just given me indicated there might be a whole horde of other people out there who would be all too glad to see Trent shuffled off this mortal coil. If my list of possible suspects could be expanded to those who weren't even involved in the brewing competition, how in the world could I ever get to the bottom of this mess?

I wouldn't allow myself to be discouraged, though. Josie was counting on me, and besides, I hated the idea of someone getting away with murder.

Not on my watch.

Since Elijah seemed open to talking...as long as he could continue to talk about how awful Trent Reynolds had been...I figured it couldn't hurt to ask.

"Do you know if he stole formulas from any of the other competitors?"

Elijah's brows drew together, and for a second,

I wondered if he was going to make something up just to make Trent look that much worse. However, he gave a reluctant shake of his head, responding, "Not that I know of. I mean, I wouldn't put it past the guy, but he wasn't involved in any other lawsuits, and even though I don't know a couple of them very well, I'm pretty sure I would have heard something if either one of those brewers had accused him of stealing from them."

"Was it that well known?" I inquired. "I mean, that Trent had built his reputation on formulas he took from other people."

"It wasn't," Elijah replied, a wry grin curling one corner of his thin lips. "But once word got out about my lawsuit, I had people coming to me in confidence and telling me they were pretty sure he'd stolen their formulas, or at least copied them and then made some very small tweaks. No one wanted to confront him openly, though. Anyway, since it wasn't a secret that I was suing Trent, I have to believe one of them would have tried to approach me at the reception and let me know he ripped them off, too."

That made sense. Or at least, since Elijah was a member of the brewing community and I wasn't, I had to believe he was a better judge of what the people in it might or might not do.

I figured I should go ahead and ask.

"Do you think any of the other competitors might have killed him?"

A long silence. Dark eyes under hooded lids met mine for a second, and then Elijah shook his head.

"I have absolutely no idea."

SIX

Motley Brew

I HEADED HOME AFTER MY INTERVIEW WITH Elijah Wright, mostly because I needed some time to process what he'd told me, but also because I was hungry and it just seemed smarter to go to the house, make myself some lunch, and decide what I wanted to do next.

While I wasn't completely shocked to learn that Trent Reynolds was a fraud—those who talked the loudest often had the most to hide—I still didn't know exactly where that put me in terms of the investigation. Unless my aura-viewing gift had gone completely sideways and was now showing me the opposite of a person's true nature, I couldn't believe that Elijah Wright had murdered Trent.

Two people to cross off my list, but three more to go. And that count was only accurate if I truly could confine my investigation to the people competing in the contest and not the apparently countless others whom Trent had either brow-beaten or outright stolen from over the past few years.

As to why someone with his means would resort to that kind of behavior, I had absolutely no idea. Nothing in the write-ups I'd read about him online had indicated he'd come from money, but to be fair, I hadn't dug very deeply, had only gone back a couple of years to get an idea of the kind of position he held in the brewing community.

It looked as though I had some more research to do.

First, though, I made myself a grilled cheese sandwich and some tomato soup, fired off a text to Calvin to let him know I was home and wasn't sure when I'd be leaving again, and then settled myself on the sofa to consume my lunch—and hand off some choice bits of melted cheddar to Sadie, who was an absolute cheese fiend and always expected to be fed those sorts of morsels whenever they were available.

Just as I was finishing up, I got a text from Josie.

We can talk to Courtney at three-thirty. Meet me at my office.

I was a bit irritated that Josie just assumed I'd be available to head over there, but the truth was, I really didn't have anything else planned for the afternoon. True, I probably should have been making plans to talk to the other competitors—David Perry, Matt Mitchell, and Nick Russell—but I didn't know how in the world I was supposed to question them about the murder when I didn't even know what to ask. Elijah Wright's lawsuit against Trent had made it easier to broach the subject with him, but clearly that was the only piece of litigation Ben Ironhorse had been able to unearth so far, meaning I'd have to try a different tack with my three remaining suspects.

If there were only three. From the sound of things, half the craft brew world seemed to be annoyed with Mr. Reynolds.

I replied to Josie and told her I'd see her at three, then headed into my office to fire up the laptop. Some quick Googling told me that Trent's parents had died in a plane crash when he was sixteen, and that he'd gone to live with an aunt until he went off to college at Arizona State University. Reading between the lines, it looked as though the family money had been kept in a trust until he turned twenty-five, at which point he started getting involved in the world of craft brewing, opening his first brewpub at twenty-seven, followed by several more.

It was still operating and apparently doing well, telling me that even if he wasn't very good at making beer, at least he did a decent job of hiring people who knew what they were doing. Part of me wanted to talk to some of his employees, just to get a read on Trent from people who weren't his direct competitors, but that first brewpub he'd opened was located all the way out in Glendale. Going back and forth would take up the greater part of four hours, and I didn't have that kind of time to burn, especially not with Josie expecting me in her office at three-thirty.

I looked over at my bookcase, at the rows of Tarot and oracle cards that took up the top two shelves. Would another reading help me now?

Maybe. Or maybe I should just try for some quickie advice.

After I closed my laptop, I went over to my altar and picked up my fluorite pendulum. I stood there for a moment, letting the pendulum dangle from my fingertips, doing my best to open myself to the universe's vibrations and any messages they might contain.

All right, then.

Is it worth talking to Trent Reynolds' employees?

The pendulum swung back and forth above the little scrying mat I used for this kind of magical working. I held myself very still so none of my movements would influence the place where it finally came to rest. Which it did a moment later, giving me an emphatic reply.

No.

So much for that. But since the pendulum seemed to be cooperating for the moment—some days, it would swing back and forth and never come to a rest, while others it would finally stop between answers, effectively giving me nothing—I figured I might as well keep trying.

Is the murderer connected to the brewing competition?

Once again, the little arrowhead-shaped piece of fluorite dangled above the mat, moving back and forth. This time, though, something seemed almost hesitant about its movements, as if it wasn't quite certain of its reply.

Sure enough, it came to a stop halfway between "no" and "yes."

It could have run out of juice, or it could be that I simply hadn't phrased the question correctly. With pendulums, sometimes it was hard to know, which was why my general go-to for this sort of thing was my trusty Tarot cards.

But at least I knew it was all right for me to stay in Globe and not go chasing all over central Arizona, trying to figure out if there any connection between Trent's employees and his sudden, terrible death. In a way, the situation felt even more awful now that I knew he was an orphan, and apparently had never married or had children. Except for that one aunt, was there even anyone left behind who would truly mourn him?

I tried to push those thoughts away, since I knew they wouldn't help me find him justice. Maybe some people would have argued that such a conniving thief didn't deserve justice, but my brain didn't work that way. It might have been my Libra rising that made me so determined to make sure this all played out fairly, or simply a need to know what had really happened. Either way, I had to get to the bottom of this.

And because I was still in Globe, that meant I had to go talk to the other three competitors.

Nick Russell was staying in the Airbnb just down the street from the one Elijah Wright currently occupied. I probably should have stopped there on my way back to the house, but at the time my brain had been filled with all the things Elijah had told me, and I'd needed a chance to stop and think and sort things out.

Like Elijah, Nick was stuck in his vacation rental while awaiting the all-clear from Henry Lewis that it was okay to go back to the competition site. The brewer also looked a little startled to see me, but he let me in anyway, probably because he thought having a chat with a stranger might be a good way to break up some of the monotony of the afternoon.

"Nah, I barely talked to Trent at all last night," Nick told me as we sat down in the living room. It wasn't as spacious as the one in the house Elijah was staying in two doors down, but still comfortable enough, with a cute electric fireplace that was currently turned on, as well as a friendly green velvet couch and matching club chair. "We sort of nodded at each other, but that's about it."

"Did you interact with him much before now?"

Nick—who apparently didn't think there was anything strange about a pregnant woman obviously not on the police force grilling him about the case—just shook his head. Probably thirty-seven or thirty-eight, he had dark blond hair and hazel eyes, and the kind of year-round tan of a person who spent a lot of time outdoors. Like the night before, he was wearing a long-sleeved Henley-style shirt, this one a sort of muddy beige color, along with jeans, although he'd traded his boots for a pair of flip-flops despite the chilly temperatures outside.

Maybe, since he was from Flagstaff, several hundred miles north of here, he thought the weather in Globe felt positively balmy.

"I saw him at some competitions," Nick said. "But because he was based in the Phoenix area and

I don't get out of northern Arizona too often, we didn't have a lot of overlap."

"You don't travel much?" I asked. "Because it seems like you brewers must—I mean, that competition where Trent Reynolds and Elijah Wright almost got into a fight was all the way over in New Mexico."

Nick just grinned. He had a small flicker of a dimple in his left cheek, somehow enhancing his laid-back vibe. Instead of asking me how I'd heard about the altercation, he only said, "Well, Trent was super-competitive, so he traveled a lot so he could enter a bunch of different contests. He had the money to do it, and that's cool. But I'm fine with staying local."

"Globe doesn't seem very local to Flagstaff," I remarked, and Nick's shoulders lifted a fraction.

"True. But the prize money for this contest was big enough that I figured it was worth the trip."

That was one topic Josie hadn't really raised with me. Had she been worried I might think she was putting too much into the competition?

"How much?" I asked.

"Ten grand," Nick replied without missing a beat. "That sort of made it all worth it."

No kidding. Josie must have put up her own money to make the competition as enticing as possible, knowing she'd have trouble getting contestants at such a late date. And while I knew she could afford it, thanks to her successful real estate business and her paid-off house, I still kind of hated that she hadn't told me how much she had riding on all this.

Because she knew you'd probably offer to cover the prize money, I thought, which was true enough. Lucien Dumond, capricious to the end, had left his millions to me and not his conniving, murderous brother or any of the acolytes in his guild. Ever since then, I'd been generous with charities and local institutions that needed a helping hand, but, thanks to a careful financial planner and accountant and lots of good investments, the money kept piling up no matter what I did.

So it was no wonder Josie might have expected me to offer to cover the event's expenses, since that was the sort of thing I did all the time. But Josie was proud—and stubborn—and didn't like taking handouts, even from her friends.

Maybe I'd bring up the matter with her...and maybe I wouldn't. Right now, it seemed more important to understand how much had been riding on this competition. Trent Reynolds might not have needed the money, but I guessed all of his fellow contestants sure did.

Which one of them was in desperate enough financial straits that they'd thought it necessary to get Trent out of the way so they'd have a better chance of winning the grand prize?

Nick Russell didn't seem all that needy to me. Sure, he'd driven down to Globe when it seemed like he was normally content to stay put in Flagstaff, but at most that was a drive of a little more than three hours. It wasn't like he'd hopped on a plane and flown halfway around the planet or anything close to it.

Which didn't mean much. His laidback exterior could be nothing more than an act designed to hide a cool, calculating brain.

Because my auras had helped me out with Elijah Wright and Sofia Barnes, I'd really been hoping they would come to my aid again and reveal something about Nick Russell. So far, though, they didn't show any sign of wanting to appear, and I did my best to quash my disappointment. After all, they'd never been super reliable, and having them actually show up twice in the same day was kind of unusual.

"I didn't kill him," Nick said, and I blinked.

"Did I say you did?"

"No," he replied, still sounding as casual as though we were discussing the sights he'd seen on his drive down south. "But I figured that's why you were here. Last night after Josie introduced you to us, Matt told me you were some kind of Nancy Drew or whatever and had solved a bunch of mysteries here in Globe."

About all I could do was blink again. "How did Matt Mitchell know about that?"

A shrug. "I guess true crime and stuff is kind of his hobby. He first heard about you after that Dillon James thing, and then he did some more research about you. Said you've kind of made the local police look like idiots."

I wasn't so sure about that. At least, I hoped Henry didn't think I made him look stupid. It wasn't his fault that he couldn't get advice from the universe the way I did. Lately, he'd been almost cordial, although I wasn't sure whether it was because he'd finally come to terms with the situation or whether Joyce had told him the important thing was that a crime had been solved, not who'd been the driving force behind finding its resolution.

"Henry Lewis is a good police chief," I said, which was true. Maybe he wasn't the world's greatest homicide detective, but that wasn't his job. On the whole, Globe was a very safe place to live, thanks in part to his oversight of the police department and the deputies he hired. "I'm glad I've been able to help him from time to time."

Another lift of Nick's shoulders. "Okay, sure. Anyway, when you showed up on my doorstep a few minutes ago, I knew you were here to ask me about Trent's murder. But I didn't have anything to do with it."

I wanted to believe him, mostly because Nick Russell definitely didn't give off creepy murder vibes, despite my auras deciding they'd done enough work today and leaving me alone on this one.

But my instincts had been wrong before. Otherwise, I would have known something was off about Melanie Knowles, even without the auras to show me her true nature.

Because Nick had been so up front about the whole thing, I thought it best to respond with equal candor.

"Do you have an alibi?"

Now he chuckled, cheerful crinkles showing around his hazel eyes. "No. From what I've heard so far, it sounds like Trent was killed sometime in the middle of the night. I was asleep...and I have a feeling you were, too. Probably, we all were."

"Except the murderer," I pointed out.

He gave a little snort of a breath, something that stopped short of being a laugh. "Yeah, except the murderer. But I talked to my girlfriend last night before I went to sleep, so at least there's a record of me being on the phone around eleven-thirty."

That was something, I supposed, although I knew the murder had occurred hours past midnight. However, I'd noticed the Airbnb had a Ring camera next to the front door, so Nick couldn't have come and gone that way without being noticed. Was there one installed by the back door as well?

Probably, just because Mavis was justifiably careful about her portfolio of vacation homes, and she'd want to make sure she had a way to keep an eye on things when they were standing vacant. There wasn't a lot of crime in Globe, but what there was tended to be the property type—burglaries, car break-ins, that kind of thing. It just made sense she'd do her best to have each of her houses protected by cameras.

In fact, there'd also been a Ring cam at the house where Elijah was staying, telling me any movements of his probably had been recorded as well. I'd knocked because I'd had too many instances of trying to use one of the devices, only to have it be out of batteries, forcing me to knock anyway when the doorbell didn't work.

"You're looking kind of discouraged," Nick remarked, and I shook my head.

"Just thinking. There's probably camera footage of each of the houses where you're staying, so it would have been hard to come and go without being recorded."

Nick ruffled his shaggy mid-brown hair. "Yeah, I noticed that Ring thing when I came here. I'm not really a fan of being surveilled, but since I'm getting put up here for free, I guess I can't exactly complain."

I supposed not. Had there been a doorbell cam at Hazel's Airbnb? Now I couldn't remember for sure—she'd had one when she was living there, which was why I was intimately acquainted with how they weren't always working if the home-owner didn't keep an eye on the battery charge, but now I couldn't recall whether she'd taken it down after she moved out.

"Anyway," Nick added, "I know there were probably a bunch of people who weren't exactly fans of Trent Reynolds, but I can't believe any of them hated him enough to kill him."

Pretty much the same thing Elijah Wright had told me, which seemed to be pointing right back to square one.

Not that I planned to give up so easily.

"Well, thanks for your input, Nick," I said, and rose from the couch. "I won't take up any more of your time."

"Not a problem," he responded, then grinned. "It's not like I'll have much to do until we're cleared to go back to our booths."

True enough. Still, I thanked him again before heading out to my car. As I slid behind the wheel—well, more like gingerly maneuvered myself, since I wanted to make sure my rounded belly had plenty of clearance—I wondered whether it was even worth my time to visit Matt Mitchell or David Perry. If their houses also had exterior cameras, then it would have been hard for them to slip out without being recorded...at least, not without it being pretty obvious that they'd tampered with the cameras in question.

I'd already talked to more than half the competitors, though, and it seemed stupid to give up at this point. There were still a couple of hours before I needed to meet Josie, and I might as well make use of them.

Even if this whole thing turned out to be an exercise in futility.

SEVEN

Here and There

SURPRISINGLY, THE DOOR OF THE AIRBNB where Matt Mitchell was staying was opened by a woman, not the man I'd been expecting. She looked as though she might be five or six years older than I was, with light brown hair pulled back into a simple ponytail and clear blue eyes.

"Can I help you?" she asked, clearly just as mystified by my presence here as I was by hers.

"Hi," I said. "My name is Selena Marx. I'm working with Josie Woodrow, the woman who's running the brewing competition."

That wasn't even a lie. I truly was working with Josie...even if not precisely in the capacity of an official of the contest.

"Oh, come on in," the woman replied. "I'm Lisa Mitchell, Matt's wife."

For a second, I stared at her, startled, before I

recovered myself. "It's nice to meet you, Lisa," I said as she ushered me into the living room. "I don't think I saw you at the reception last night."

"Oh, I was there, but I didn't come in with Matt," she explained. "We ran over a nail as we were driving to the reception, so I stayed in the parking lot and waited for Triple-A to show up while he went inside. I told him this whole thing was about him and not me, so it didn't make any sense for him to wait for the tow truck."

"And I told her I could put on the spare and we didn't need to call Triple-A, but she insisted," Matt Mitchell put in as he emerged from the hallway that I guessed led to the small home's bathroom and bedrooms.

Lisa waved a hand. "And have you get your one decent pair of jeans dirty? I don't think so." She paused there, then asked, "Can I get you something? A glass of water? And please, have a seat."

"Some water would be great," I told her, since Nick hadn't offered me any when I was over at his Airbnb, and I was starting to feel pretty thirsty.

She excused herself to go to the kitchen, while I sat down on the small beige-upholstered couch and Matt looked at me with what appeared to be an odd mixture of amusement and wariness.

"I was wondering when you were going to drop by," he said, and I tilted my head, glad I'd already resolved to be utterly truthful about my involvement in the investigation.

"Nick said you were into true crime," I replied. "I guess I should be flattered that you've heard of me."

"Well, the Dillon James case was kind of crazy," Matt said. He took a seat on a small armless chair placed to the right of the couch, just as Lisa returned with a glass of water and handed it over to me.

"There you go."

I thanked her and took a sip, letting the water slide down my dry throat. Yes, that was much better.

"Ms. Marx is here to talk to me about Trent's murder," Matt offered, and Lisa immediately frowned.

"It's terrible," she said. "I'm kind of surprised Ms. Woodrow is going ahead with the competition after what happened."

"Josie doesn't let a whole lot stop her," I observed wryly. "But I'm trying to help by doing my best to get this whole mess figured out before the contest starts tomorrow."

This admission made her shoot me a startled glance, while Matt just nodded, as if he'd already guessed that was why Josie had me on the case.

"I'm not sure there's much we can tell you—"

Lisa began, but her husband broke in before she could get any further.

"But she still wants to hear it anyway," he said, fixing me with a pair of keen gray eyes.

"I do," I said, since I couldn't really deny that was the whole reason for me being here in the first place.

Matt smiled, but there wasn't much humor in his expression. "We left the reception around ten o'clock and came straight back here. I'm sure Mavis's cameras recorded our arrival time, if you want to double-check that."

For a moment, I wondered how he even knew who Mavis was, then guessed that Josie must have mentioned her name to him. My friend did have a tendency to spill every bit of trivia she possessed when she was talking to someone new, as if she thought that was the best way to get them caught up on everything that was happening in Globe.

"That's okay," I said evenly. "I believe you."

"Then we got up this morning and went to have some breakfast," Lisa added. "It wasn't until we got back here and Matt was getting ready to head back over to the site that we heard from Josie, telling us what had happened."

"I've been thinking about it," Matt said. He rubbed a hand across a chin that definitely hadn't been shaved this morning, and maybe not the day before, either. "I wish I could say I was surprised that someone killed Trent, but considering how many people he got into it with, it's not that much of a shocker."

Possibly a jaded view of the situation, and yet I wouldn't bother to argue with him, not after what I'd heard from Elijah about Trent Reynolds' questionable business practices. "You knew about him stealing people's beer recipes?"

Because neither Lisa nor Matt looked too surprised by my question, I had to believe they'd already heard those accusations.

"I did," Matt said. "I mean, he never took any of mine—I also make sure to add a little something extra to make it hard to rip off one of my formulas —but there was that incident with him and Elijah in Ruidoso, and I heard rumors about problems with other people, too."

Right. I remembered that Matt Mitchell had given up a lucrative career in pharmaceuticals to become a craft brewer, so it made sense that he had a much better handle on the chemistry-related side of the business than a lot of other people might. "What other people?" I asked then. "Anyone at this competition?"

"No," Matt replied. "Not that I heard of, anyway, besides Elijah. There was some bad blood between him and the guys who run a microbrewery up in Payson, but they're not competing this weekend."

Again, pretty on par with what Elijah Wright had already told me. "He stole their formulas?"

"Allegedly," Matt said. "They settled out of court, though, so I have a feeling Trent was guilty as hell and just wanted to pay to make it all go away."

Lisa had been listening to this back-and-forth between Matt and me, a worried little pucker pulling at her neatly arched brows. Now, though, she said to her husband, "But they wouldn't have any reason to go after him now, right? I mean, he paid the settlement."

"I suppose they wouldn't," he replied, although the words came out slowly, as if he was trying to think it through as he spoke. "I'm not saying they're not still plenty pissed off at him. I just don't think they'd have much of a reason to kill him. Besides, the Linderhof brothers aren't killers any more than I am...than any of us are."

I made a mental note of the name—which wasn't too difficult—although I guessed if I tried to follow that particular trail to Payson, it would only lead to yet another dead end.

"Also, the way he was killed," Matt went on. "It was clearly premeditated. No one fills a vat that's supposed to be only a prop full of water and then drowns a person in it without planning the whole thing beforehand. Whoever it was, they wanted to make sure it was an ugly death."

One might have said that any death by murder was ugly. But drowning was very different from being shot in the head. You took longer to die, meaning you probably had a lot more time to think about what was happening to you...and why.

I shuddered, and Lisa's expression was bleak. Maybe she and her husband had already discussed all this, and she was hearing things for the second time that she really hadn't wanted to contemplate during the first go-'round.

Matt fixed me with another of those scalpel-sharp looks. Right then, I could see why he might have been interested in true crime—it was a way of keeping his clever, active brain engaged in a manner that was very different from formulating a new lager or ale. "Have you heard anything from the police?"

"Nothing more than you probably have," I replied. "I mean, I heard about Trent's death from Josie, so she was basically passing along what she learned from Chief Lewis. Right now, I think a lot of what happened is a mystery. Unfortunately, there aren't any surveillance cameras at the old high school because the place is kind of semi-retired. We host a special event there every once in a while, but there just wasn't any money in the city budget to install a real security system like there is at the new high school. I think the town figured the chain-link fence would be enough to keep casual trespassers out, and there wasn't much reason to break in otherwise."

"So, there's no way to find out who went into the gym last night?" Lisa asked. She was still frowning slightly, telling me she didn't much like anything she was hearing.

Her husband responded before I could decide how to answer. "They'll probably be checking local traffic cameras and that kind of stuff to see if they can get an idea of who was driving in that area around the time in question. But if the killer came in on foot, then he's going to be harder to track down."

That was for sure. I hadn't even thought about viewing the traffic camera footage to see if they'd recorded anything of use, but then, it wasn't like I was a trained detective or something, or even someone like Matt, with an interest in true crime. As far as I was concerned, my adopted hometown had plenty of true crime of its own.

And to be honest, I wasn't even sure whether Globe had traffic cameras. If it did, then they were very inconspicuous, since I couldn't remember ever noticing one of them.

Another question occurred to me. "Was it common knowledge that Trent stole from other brewers?"

"No," Matt said immediately. "Otherwise, he would have been put out of business. I don't know the details, but it sounds like part of the settlement with the Linderhofs was that they couldn't talk about what had happened."

"You knew about it, though," I replied.

Now he smiled a little. "Well," he said, "sometimes people say things they shouldn't after they've had a couple of beers...or four or five. But I haven't talked about the settlement with anyone except Lisa...and you, but you already knew about the situation with Trent."

His wife had been listening to this entire exchange intently, but as Matt paused, she commented, "And his brewpubs are really nice. The stolen beer formula thing is problematic, I know, but when you go to one of Trent's restaurants, you have a good experience. The food is great, and they also offer some local Arizona wines for those of us who aren't big beer drinkers."

That remark made me smile a little. "You're not into beer?"

"Not really," she responded, and Matt offered me a rueful grin of his own.

"I guess that's the irony of the situation," he said, then leaned over so he could press a kiss against her cheek. "But since Lisa's pretty much perfect in every other way, I've decided to overlook that small character flaw."

Those words made her give him a little mock-punch in the arm, and they exchanged a goofy smile. Looking at them, I knew I didn't need my auras to help me with this particular character judgment.

Matt Mitchell wasn't any guiltier of Trent Reynolds' murder than I was.

The last stop on my little tour of possible suspects was the vacation rental where David Perry was staying. That house was the newest addition to Mavis's stable of Airbnbs, and wasn't located in the older section of Globe, with its cute cottages and carefully restored farmhouse-style homes, but in a subdivision on the hillside to the east of the town... the same neighborhood where Nora Lemmon had once lived with her murderous husband.

But he was safely locked up in the maximum-security prison in Florence, about eighty miles from Globe, and Nora had sold the house and bought a condo in Tempe, where she could be closer to her two daughters. There was nothing left of them here except some bitter memories.

All the same, I couldn't help experiencing a little shiver as I parked my Renegade in front of the vacation rental and turned off the engine. True, Nora's house had been two streets over, but since all the homes in this subdivision resembled one another strongly, in the sort of cookie-cutter ersatz

Mediterranean style that had been popular in the 1990s, the memory of what she'd endured while living here was still almost overpowering.

However, I told myself Nora's tragedies didn't have anything to do with the reason why I was here today, and besides, she'd started her life over, was happy and thriving, the last I heard.

That was why I walked briskly up the little flagstone path that led to the front door of the Airbnb where David Perry was staying, and wouldn't let myself hesitate before reaching out and knocking twice.

No reply after a moment or two passed, and I frowned. Well, maybe Mr. Perry preferred his guests to use the Ring camera that was affixed to the doorframe.

Fine. I pushed the button and waited, and still no reply. Then an automated voice said, "I'm sorry, we can't come to the door right now. Please leave a message."

Great. Now a door had to sound like someone's voicemail?

Although I knew the camera was probably recording my every movement, I still didn't want to give away everything. So I just said, "I'm sorry I missed you. I'll try again later," and then turned away from the door and headed down the walkway toward my Renegade. Luckily, the house had some neatly trimmed euphorbia hedges that blocked most of the view of the street, so I didn't think I had to worry about the camera picking up my license plate or anything.

Still, I couldn't help feeling annoyed as I drove away, even as I tried to tell myself David Perry wasn't under house arrest or anything close to it. All Henry had said was that the contestants needed to stay in Globe, which meant Mr. Perry could be downtown having lunch, exploring the local Walmart, or even taking a hike somewhere, although that sort of activity would be stretching the letter of the police chief's edicts just a bit. Some of our local hiking trails were within town limits, but not many of them.

Well, I could always stop by the store and see how Hazel was doing, and maybe poke my head in to have a chat with Archie. Or maybe not; Fridays were his second-busiest days, and I realized he was probably teaching a class. Dropping in to Victoria's studio also was a no-go, because even though her design business was on a regular Monday through Friday schedule, she'd finished her last project for the year and was probably in the studio with Archie, stealing some extra time with her husband while also assisting him with his students.

All right, the shop it was. Besides, once I'd killed enough time, I could just walk down the street to Josie's office and not have to move my car.

With my plan settled, I parked in the lot behind

the shop, then got out and headed inside. When I'd first bought the store and the accompanying apartment upstairs, there had only been a private rear entrance opening onto a short hallway that connected to the storeroom. Now, though, the entrance had been expanded into an actual foyer, with stairs on one side leading up to Victoria's studio, and a door with a pretty etched glass insert with a crescent moon and the name of the shop written above it directly ahead so people could come and go through both entrances.

Because I'd noticed the parking lot was fairly full, I wasn't too surprised to see quite a few people browsing the store's wares, and Hazel with a line of three people waiting to check out. She didn't look exactly harried, but I could tell she would much rather have been at home with her paints and easel than spending her afternoon dealing with holiday shoppers.

I waved at her as I came in and mouthed, "Do you need help?"

She shook her head. To be fair, there was only the one cash register and credit card processor, so there wasn't a lot I could have done to ease the backup at the counter.

But I was able to move around the store and offer advice or clarification to several shoppers who weren't quite sure what they needed, and at least that saved Hazel from having to answer questions while also helping people check out. The flurry of activity subsided about five minutes after I got there, and my friend let out a sigh of relief.

"I was thinking it was going to be quiet today, and then that busload of tourists pulled up." She stopped there, brows drawing together. "Is everything okay? I figured you were going to be running all over town, tracking down clues."

"Well, I was," I replied. "I've talked to all the contestants in the brewing competition, except for Dave Perry. He wasn't at the Airbnb when I stopped by, so I thought I'd swing over here and see how you were doing before I meet Josie at three-thirty." I paused, then added, "I don't suppose you've seen him."

Hazel's nose scrunched slightly, as though she was trying to dredge up a slippery memory. "He was the one with the man-bun, right?"

I nodded.

"Then he hasn't been by here," she said. "You think he took off?"

"I doubt it," I said. "I'm sure he just got bored and figured he'd do some exploring around town. Anyway, he was kind of my last hope of finding someone who seems guilty, because no one else among the possible suspects is pinging my 'guilty' radar at all."

"That's a bummer," Hazel responded, then gave a rueful shake of her head. "I mean, I suppose it's good that none of them is a murderer, but still, it would have made life easier for everyone involved if you'd been able to pin it on one of the people you talked to."

No kidding. However, both Sofia Barnes' and Elijah Wright's auras told me they weren't killers, and Nick Russell seemed way too laid-back to hate someone enough that he thought drowning him in a brewing vat was a good way of getting rid of a rival. Matt Mitchell had been a bit more of a wild card, but again, the way he'd interacted with his wife made me think he was a good person and definitely not a murderer, either.

Which left the elusive Mr. Perry as my one and only possible lead.

"So, why're you meeting Josie?" Hazel asked next, and I sighed a little.

"We're going to talk to Courtney Hill, the girl who was working the coat check at the reception," I replied. "I'm hoping she might have noticed something unusual, because right now, the most plausible explanation for how the killer got into the facility unnoticed is that he managed to steal the key from Josie's bag and have it duplicated without anyone noticing."

"That seems like kind of a stretch," Hazel remarked.

Didn't I know it. Unfortunately, it was the only explanation that made any sense.

Or...was it? Henry claimed there hadn't been any signs of forced entry, but I didn't know enough about picking locks to have any idea exactly what to look for, only that a skilled locksmith might be able to tell that a lock had been tampered with.

Maybe Calvin would know.

"Hang on," I told Hazel. "I just thought of something."

I fired off a quick text to my husband about lock picking. He must have been in his office rather than out on patrol, because he answered almost at once.

A forensic locksmith could probably find concrete signs that the lock was picked. But it's not something most people would be able to see, not even Henry.

Do we have any forensic locksmiths in Globe?

I couldn't see my husband, obviously, but I had to believe he smiled as he read my message.

No. We'd have to send for someone in Phoenix. I can have one of my deputies start searching, if you want.

Yes, I did want. Or rather, even though I would go ahead with the interview with Courtney as planned, that didn't mean I wouldn't also look for someone who could independently verify that the lock to the old gymnasium had in fact been picked.

That would be great.

Okay. I'll let you know when we find someone. You holding up okay?

Talking to people. Trying to figure this out. I'm all right.

Texting definitely didn't have a lot of space for expressing emotions, but I guessed some of my tiredness must have seeped through, because his next message made me feel a teeny bit better.

Then let me take you out for a steak at the Gold Dust. You've got enough on your plate without worrying about dinner.

Oh, how I loved that man of mine. True, a steak dinner would've been even better with a bottle of cab to go along with it, but I'd make that sacrifice.

Sounds perfect.

He told me again he'd let me know when he'd found someone who could come out to Globe to look at the locks, and that was the end of the convo.

I looked up to see Hazel's curious expression. "Well?" she asked.

"We're going to see if we can find a forensic locksmith to take a look at the locks at the gym," I explained. "Honestly, I don't know why Henry didn't think of that."

Her mouth pursed. "Well, Henry's a decent guy, but he's not exactly long on imagination. His own inspection didn't find any evidence of tampering, ergo, there wasn't any." She hesitated, then asked, "Do you really think he'll let you have an outside expert look at the site? Has it even been cleared?"

No, it hadn't, last I'd heard, but I figured Josie could fill me in on the status of the crime scene when I met with her. "I don't know," I replied. "But I'm sure it will be soon, if it hasn't already. And I'm pretty sure Josie will overrule Henry if he has any objections to having a forensic locksmith look at the place."

For a second, Hazel's lips parted slightly, as if she was about to ask whether Josie had the authority to boss around the police chief when it came to an investigation taking place in his jurisdiction. But then my friend seemed to remember that even Henry Lewis had a hard time standing up to Josie when she got dug in about something, so Hazel apparently abandoned any protests she'd been about to make.

"Well, I hope you find something," she said, her tone neutral.

So did I. And since it was now almost a quarter after three, I figured it was time for me to walk down to Josie's office and wait for Courtney Hill to arrive.

I could only hope Josie would be as excited about the prospect of having a forensic locksmith look into the case as I was.

EIGHT

The Case of the Purloined Key

Luckily, Josie seemed even more thrilled by the concept of a forensic locksmith than I had been. "That would be an enormous help!" she exclaimed. Then her expression sobered a little, and she added, "Do you think we still need to talk to Courtney?"

"Absolutely," I replied at once. "Even if it turns out the lock was picked, that doesn't mean Courtney might not have seen something unusual at the reception. After all, she interacted with almost every single person who came through the door last night, and even if she might not have realized she witnessed something strange at the time, she still could let us know about it."

"True," Josie agreed. "I'll admit, I was so busy greeting everyone and keeping an eye on the caterers that I'm sure I could have missed something."

I actually thought it highly more likely that I might have overlooked anything unusual, just because I was focused on my own group of friends and not paying much attention to the other attendees. But I only nodded and said I supposed that was possible, and right after that exchange, someone knocked at Josie's office door.

She went ahead and opened it, even though I was standing a little closer. Just outside in the reception area—although Josie had never actually had a receptionist during the time I'd known her, preferring to handle everything herself—was Courtney Hill, looking much more casual today than she had the night before, when she'd been wearing a pretty green velvet dress instead of the jeans and hoodie she had on now.

From the startled flicker in her blue eyes, I guessed she hadn't been expecting to see me here, and that Josie had withheld the information from her on purpose. I knew I'd never seen Courtney in my shop, telling me she was probably from the kind of strict family who didn't want their daughter going into a witchy store like mine.

But that was neither here nor there. I didn't care what her family thought of Once in a Blue Moon. No, I only wanted to know if she'd seen anything strange at the reception the night before.

"Hello, Courtney," Josie said in breezy tones, moving right past the awkward moment as though it had never occurred at all. "This is my friend Selena. She's helping me find out what happened to Trent Reynolds last night."

"Hi, Courtney," I said, and she mumbled a greeting before sitting down in the chair Josie offered her.

However, once Courtney had the relative safety of the chair to support her, she seemed to gather enough courage to say, "I don't know if there's much I can tell you. I really didn't see anything strange. I mean, it was just a bunch of grown-ups talking and drinking."

Despite myself, I couldn't quite hold back a smile. Yes, to a teenage observer, that's exactly what the evening would have looked like.

"Oh, there must have been something," Josie persisted, and Courtney just shrugged. In her hoodie and jeans, her only makeup a little lip gloss, she looked a lot younger and less sure of herself than the poised young woman I'd seen the night before.

"Well, I noticed that one of the guys' wives came in later than he did," the girl volunteered. "But then I saw a tow truck go driving past right after that, so I guessed they must have had car trouble or something."

"They did," I agreed. Courtney's comments

appeared to verify that Matt and Lisa Mitchell's story had been true...not that I'd really suspected it wasn't. "There wasn't anything else, though?"

She hesitated for so long that at first I wasn't sure whether she was going to reply at all. "Well...."

"It's all right," Josie said, obviously trying to adopt what she thought were soothing tones. "You can tell us anything."

Courtney's big blue eyes were full of worry. "And you won't tell my parents?"

From the other side of the chair where the girl sat, Josie's eyes met mine, questioning, even though about all I could do was give a very small lift of my shoulders. It seemed we were both mystified as to what Courtney's parents had to do with any of this.

However, once she began to speak again, the pieces of the puzzle started to fall into place.

"My boyfriend Justin came by a little before eight," she explained. "He knew I was working at the reception, even though I told him not to come over because I'd be busy. But we never get to see each other at night—my parents don't believe in dating, so we just see each other at school and maybe on Saturday afternoons when they think I'm at the movies with friends."

"So, Justin showed up," Josie said, and Courtney nodded.

"I know I shouldn't have gone off with him, but honestly, pretty much everyone who was coming to the reception had gotten there by then. It didn't seem like a big deal, because I'd already told Justin I had to be back in the coatroom when people started to leave."

No, she'd probably rationalized to herself that it was fine to slip away for fifteen or twenty minutes or whatever, and to find a dark corner where she could engage in the exact sort of behavior her parents were obviously trying very hard to prevent.

Josie's expression was disapproving in the extreme, although I had a feeling that was more because of the way the girl had abandoned her post than because she cared about a little teenage necking. I gave the faintest of head shakes, hoping my friend would recognize the gesture as my way of letting her know she shouldn't act too critical for fear Courtney might decide to clam up completely.

It seemed the message got through, because when Josie spoke again, her tone was gentle enough. "I can see that," she said. "There was a big chunk of time in the middle of the reception when you didn't have much to do."

"Exactly," Courtney responded at once, her expression relieved. "I would never have slipped off with Justin if I thought anyone else was going to show up. In fact, I waited about ten minutes to make sure no one was coming late. But they didn't, so we went out to his car and...."

The words trailed off, and her cheeks flushed bright pink.

Well, I wasn't about to ask her exactly what she'd been up to, and neither, it seemed was Josie. Skipping past all that, she said, "Do you know how long you were gone?"

Courtney's cheeks were now almost fuchsia. "Um...I'm not sure. Maybe a half hour or a little more?"

Once again, Josie and I exchanged a significant glance. Globe wasn't a very big town; a half hour... well, let's say forty minutes or even more, as I had a feeling Courtney was fudging the numbers a bit... would definitely be sufficient time to steal the gymnasium keys from Josie's purse, drive over to Walmart and use the kiosk there to duplicate them, and then return to the reception site and deposit the stolen keys back in her bag with no one the wiser.

I could tell my friend was thinking pretty much the exact same thing I was. However, since we still didn't know for sure whether the killer had actually taken Josie's keys or whether he'd picked the locks instead, there wasn't much point in giving Courtney grief over her carelessness. She was only a sixteen-year-old girl after all, and would have had no idea that someone with murder on their mind might have used her thoughtless behavior as a way of accomplishing their goal.

"You're not going to tell my parents, are you?" she asked, misinterpreting our silence. "They'll kill me if they find out I was with Justin last night!"

"No, we're not going to tell your parents," Josie assured her. "We're just trying to figure out how Trent Reynolds was able to get into the gym late last night after everything was locked up, and we think maybe he came into the coat check area and borrowed the key from my purse."

It didn't escape my notice that she'd made it sound as though Trent was the one who'd taken the keys, not the murderer. In fact, the more I thought about it, the more that particular scenario made sense. After all, Trent had gotten into the gym somehow. Or at least, I assumed that was what had happened the night before, because, barring further information after the medical examiner's report was complete, there didn't seem to be any sign that he'd been murdered someplace else and then dumped in the vat of water.

Courtney now looked pale, the embarrassed flush from a few minutes earlier gone as if it had never been there at all. "Oh, my God," she whispered. "It's my fault he was murdered."

"Of course it isn't," Josie said briskly. "You didn't hand those keys to him. All you did was give him an opportunity to take them. But it wouldn't have mattered that you'd left the coat check area unguarded if he hadn't already had the intention to take my keys."

This no-nonsense explanation made Courtney look a little less ill at ease, although I could tell she was still mentally beating herself up for allowing her boyfriend to lure her away from her post. "I'm really sorry," she said.

"It's okay," I put in. No matter what self-recriminations Courtney currently had running through her head, Josie was right. It wasn't the girl's fault that Trent...or the killer...had taken her keys. "We just wanted to figure out how it could have happened."

An unwilling nod. Then Courtney said, "Can I go now? I told my mom I had a meeting with one of my teachers after class today, but if I'm too late getting home, she's going to start asking a lot of questions."

"Of course," Josie replied at once. "We don't want you getting in any trouble."

After giving a relieved nod, the girl hefted her backpack, which she'd left leaning against a leg of her chair, and then hurried out of Josie's office. The two of us looked at each other for a moment.

Josie opened her mouth as if to say something,

but her iPhone—in a sparkly red case, naturally—
rang from its spot on her desk right then. She
looked down at the screen, mouthed "Henry" at
me, then picked it up.

"Hi, Henry," she said and paused, telling me
he'd probably started speaking immediately and
hadn't bothered with any preliminaries. Because
of that, there wasn't much for me to listen to on
my end, only Josie making "mm-hmm" noises
from time to time. At the end, though, she
managed to say, "Thank you, Henry. That's all
good to know."

And then she ended the call and set the phone
back down on her desk.

"Well?" I prompted.

"That was Henry," Josie replied, quite unnecessarily. "He wanted to let me know the crime scene
has been cleared and that I—and the contestants—
can go back in whenever we like. Also, he just got
the coroner's preliminary report."

My ears pricked up immediately. This wasn't
information the police chief would have voluntarily
shared with me, but Josie obviously had zero
compunction about passing on what she'd learned.

"There was a struggle of some kind," she
continued. "The medical examiner found bruising
on Trent Reynolds' face, as though someone had
punched him several times. Also, he had marks on
his neck that seemed to indicate someone had

choked him, although the cause of death was determined to be drowning."

She paused there, head tilted toward me, as though expecting some kind of response.

What I was supposed to say, I didn't know. All I could think of was Trent struggling with his assailant, who must have begun to throttle him and then realized he wanted his victim to drown rather than choke to death.

"That's...awful," I managed.

Josie nodded, her expression more sober now. "It does sound terrible," she replied. "And the bruises explain why there were signs of a struggle. He must have fought with the killer, and that was when all those bottles got knocked down from the shelves in his display area."

I could almost see it in my mind's eye—the two men fighting, Trent doing his best to get the upper hand but eventually failing. Whoever the killer was, he must have been in good shape and very strong, because Trent Reynolds wasn't the sort of person you could imagine being easily overcome in a physical confrontation.

Which meant there was absolutely no way Sofia Barnes could be the murderer. I'd already pretty much come to that conclusion, but the medical examiner's report seemed to make it crystal clear.

And if Trent had given even half of what he'd

gotten, then you'd think the killer would be sporting wounds of his own from the altercation. I definitely hadn't noticed any bruises or cuts or scrapes on Matt Mitchell or Elijah Wright. Nick Russell had a couple of scrapes on the knuckles of his left hand, but I'd assumed the minor injuries had occurred while he was bottling some beer, or maybe when he was out hiking or snowboarding or whatever he did up in Flagstaff to maintain that year-'round tan.

But maybe those scrapes warranted a closer look.

Problem was, I didn't have any idea how to casually ask Nick if I could see the wounds on his hand. We'd already had our talk and I hadn't learned anything substantive, so in his mind, he probably thought we didn't have any further business.

Unless....

"So, if the scene's cleared, you're going to let everyone back into the site, right?"

Josie nodded. "Yes, I was just about to send a text to the group telling them to meet me there at four."

Perfect. "Mind if I tag along?"

She didn't hesitate for a second. After all, she had even more riding on this than I did.

"Not at all."

The only person who appeared surprised to see me show up at Josie's side when everyone convened at the old high school's gymnasium was David Perry, probably because he was the sole member of the group I hadn't yet been able to visit. To my relief, Josie took some of the awkwardness out of the situation—or maybe made it worse—by going straight up to him and saying, "Hi, David. My friend Selena is helping me with finding out who killed Trent. Do you mind talking to her for a moment?"

He blinked. The man-bun seemed to be reserved for formal occasions, because today he had his long brown hair pulled back into a ponytail, and he was dressed casually like everyone else— jeans and a long-sleeved T-shirt, work boots.

His gaze flickered for just a second at my bulging midsection, and he seemed to do a quick mental calculus before saying, "I've got a lot to do—"

"This won't take long," I broke in. "Really, I just need five minutes."

A tightening of his mouth, followed by, "Are you a private detective?"

"Um…sort of," I said. "I've helped Josie with a lot of investigations."

Just the teeniest of lies. True, the majority of my inquiries into the murder and mayhem that had occurred in Globe since I'd moved here hadn't been for her direct benefit, but because all those mysteries had been tied up in a neat little bow, I supposed they had helped her promote the town and let people know it really was a safe place to live.

David Perry still didn't look very convinced. However, he didn't exactly say no, but instead replied, "Well, we can talk while I get things set up."

"Sure," I said at once. I would have preferred his undivided attention, but talking to him at all was better than nothing.

The other four contestants had already gone off to their individual display booths, so I followed David to his, which was set up at the end of the row. It was the one Victoria had designed in a sort of industrial farmhouse style, with white-painted cabinets and butcher-block countertops and black iron handles on the cupboards.

I wondered where she'd gotten all this stuff on such short notice but reminded myself that she had lots of connections in the industry, and had probably used leftovers from previous design jobs or asked around at local suppliers to see if they had any odd job lots she could use. As David began to pull bottles of beer out of one of the cases sitting on the floor by a set of open shelves, I figured I might as well ask.

"What time did you leave the reception last night?"

He was halfway turned away from me, so all I could see was one side of his mouth as it lifted in a wry smile. "Right to the point, huh?"

"I told you I only needed five minutes."

Without pausing, he said, "I left as things were wrapping up. So...around ten, I think."

"And I assume people saw you leave," I replied.

"There weren't too many left by then," he said. "Josie, and that blonde girl who was doing the coat check."

A certain flicker in his blue eyes told me he'd noticed Courtney...and probably wished she was a few years older.

Doing my best to push that uncomfortable thought aside, I said, "Do you have anyone who can corroborate your whereabouts after that?"

Now he paused, hands on his hips. I could tell there weren't any bruises or scrapes on those hands —or anywhere else that was visible—telling me he probably wasn't our culprit. Still, I wasn't going to stop asking questions, not when we'd just gotten started.

A lazy smile playing around his lips, he said, "Yeah, I do. A woman named Amber Drummond. Know her?"

I shook my head. Globe was a small town, barely seven thousand residents, but if someone hadn't crossed my orbit for whatever reason, then they'd still be a stranger to me even after I'd lived here for almost three years.

"Nice gal," David commented. "Anyway, we talked during the reception, and then we went back to her place."

Which probably explained why he hadn't been there this morning when I knocked on the door of the Airbnb where he was staying. He sounded completely casual about the whole thing, and I told myself I shouldn't be too surprised. Just because I wasn't into one-night stands didn't mean there weren't plenty of people out there who had no problem with them.

And besides, I'd already heard rumors that David Perry was kind of a player.

"Do you want Amber's number?" he said with a sly smile. "I mean, I already gave her info to your police chief, but—"

"No, that's fine," I cut in hastily. "I believe you. I just want to get this straightened out for everyone's sakes."

"It does kind of suck," he agreed. "I'm glad we're going ahead with the competition, but I know Josie's not happy that she has this murder situation hanging over the whole thing."

"Not happy" was kind of an understatement, but yes, unless I came up with an answer in the next twenty-four hours, she'd just have to go ahead and do her best to acknowledge the tragedy while still convincing people that attending the High Country Brewing Competition was a good idea.

"Well, thanks for being so honest with me," I said. "I'll let you get back to work."

And with that, I headed back to the spot where Josie stood, phone in hand while she whipped off a quick text and the contestants continued to work on their various booths. After she was done with the text, she slipped her phone into her purse and gave me an expectant look.

"Anything useful?" she asked.

"Not really," I replied. "That is, David Perry has a rock-solid alibi, as far as I can tell. He claims he was with a woman named Amber Drummond all night. Do you know her?"

At once, Josie's lips pinched with disapproval. "Well, 'know' is probably an exaggeration. We've crossed paths a couple of times, but we don't really move in the same circles. She's a waitress at the Drift Inn."

The Drift Inn was a kind of dive-y bar a few blocks down Bridge Street from my shop. That part of town hadn't really been gentrified yet, and the Inn seemed to be the nexus for whatever groups of bikers came through town while driving down Highway 187. If Amber Drummond really worked there, I could see why she might not have enlisted Josie for real estate advice or shown up at a city council meeting to voice her concerns about a planned piece of road work.

What she'd been doing at the reception, I had no idea. I hadn't been involved in any of the planning, so I didn't know exactly how Josie had invited people, since I kind of doubted she'd hand-delivered every invitation the way she had with me. Then again, it wouldn't have been very hard to crash the event, since she'd been busy introducing people and basically making the circuit while Courtney was left to watch the door.

And there had been that big gap of time when the girl hadn't even been checking people's coats, but had sneaked off to be with her boyfriend. I supposed it was entirely plausible that Amber had arrived then and had slipped into the reception with no one even noticing.

However she'd gotten in, it sounded like she'd made a beeline for David Perry...or maybe it was the other way around, and he'd noticed her because she was one of the few single women there.

"Attractive enough, I suppose," Josie added, although something in her tone told me she didn't think much of anyone who would be attracted to the likes of Amber Drummond.

Since I hadn't seen her for myself, I couldn't comment. "Well, she gave David Perry a great alibi, so I think we can scratch him off our list."

A list that effectively had zero suspects on it,

except for maybe Nick Russell, the other brewer from Flagstaff.

"But I need to talk to Nick," I added. "After that, I suppose I'll just go on home, since I've already spoken with everyone."

The disapproving expression Josie had worn while we were discussing Amber Drummond abruptly shifted to one of worry. "You mean you've already exhausted all leads?"

"Pretty much," I replied. I didn't like telling her that, but it was the simple truth. "Right now, I don't think any of the competitors is our killer. But I want to check on one thing."

She nodded, face still tight and anxious. I knew she was trying to soldier her way through this as best she could, and yet I realized she must be understandably worried that the whole thing was going to collapse if I couldn't locate Trent Reynolds' murderer.

Because of that, she didn't protest when I excused myself and went over to Nick Russell's booth. His resembled a traditional pub, with dark wood cabinets and green marble countertops. He was in the middle of doing something complicated with a beaker and a setup that looked like something right out of my high school chemistry class, so I waited off to one side until he was done.

"Oh, hi, Selena," he said when he glanced up.

Clearly, he hadn't expected to see me standing right there. "Help you with something?"

I glanced down at the scrapes on his left hand. "I was just wondering about those."

And I nodded toward the scabs on his knuckles.

"They're not from punching Trent Reynolds in the face, if that's what you're asking," Nick replied. "A couple of days before I came down here, I helped a friend replace the radiator in his truck. It was kind of tight quarters, so I lost a little skin."

I'd already guessed it must have been something like that, but I still wished he hadn't had such an easy explanation to offer for the wounds on his hands. "And I suppose your friend can back up that story."

"Sure." Nick paused there, one hand reaching up to push a strand of sun-lightened hair away from his face. As he did so, his aura wavered into existence around him, a friendly, sunshiny kind of yellow. I'd seen some auras that were a sickly version of the same color, showing guilt and bad feelings and much more, but this wasn't that sort of yellow. No, it was the kind of shade you might paint your kitchen if you wanted to be cheered up every morning when you walked in.

Someone who was a murderer definitely wouldn't have an aura that color.

It seemed like a final sign from the universe

that I was definitely barking up the wrong tree here, skinned knuckles or no.

"Do you want to talk to him personally?" Nick asked, and I shook my head.

"No," I said. "I believe you."

Which meant I really had been telling Josie the truth.

My current list of suspects was effectively zero.

NINE

Breaking Glass

BY THE TIME I GOT BACK TO THE HOUSE, IT was a little after five. Perfect, because Calvin would be home soon, and I could talk to him about my frustrating and disappointing day and get the encouragement I desperately needed.

As often happened when I was feeling cranky and stymied, I went into the kitchen and rooted around in the fridge and the cupboard, hoping that figuring out dinner might make me feel a little better about life. That was why, when Calvin got home about fifteen minutes later, I was just finishing frying bacon for a batch of homemade carbonara sauce.

He bent down and kissed me as Sadie danced around his feet, waiting for her turn to get some love. His expression was surprised. "You're making dinner after all? I thought we were going out tonight."

Oops. I'd been so focused on trying to figure out who had really killed Trent Reynolds, it had completely slipped my mind that Calvin had offered to take me to the restaurant at the casino. I gave him an apologetic smile and said, "I was hoping making dinner might help to settle my nerves."

His head tilted a little as he studied my face. "I guess your day didn't go the way you wanted it to."

"That's putting it mildly." I laid the last two pieces of bacon on a plate covered in a paper towel so they would drain, then turned back toward my husband. "I have a long list of suspects and no leads. Or rather, I *thought* I had suspects, but they either have watertight alibis, or my auras are telling me they can't be the killer."

"It's good that your auras are helping, though, right?" my husband ventured.

"Maybe," I said, knowing my tone sounded a little sulky. "But I'd rather they were showing me murderous auras so I'd know who the killer is."

Calvin actually chuckled at that comment. "Well, I suppose that would make the situation a little simpler. Still, it's not a bad thing to be crossing people off your list. At least that way, you won't waste time and energy going after prospects that don't pan out."

I supposed he had a point. Figuring I'd spent enough time complaining, I said, "Were you able to find a forensic locksmith?"

He nodded. "Yes, but he can't be at the site until noon tomorrow. That's why it's probably a good idea to keep investigating all other avenues until we can learn for sure whether or not the lock at the gym was picked."

"It might not have been," I said, and told him how Josie and I had discovered that Courtney Hill hadn't been watching the door the entire time at the reception, giving someone an easy opening to go in and steal the keys from Josie's purse. "And then whoever took the keys could just go to the kiosk at Walmart and get a duplicate and that would be the end of it," I finished.

At once, Calvin shook his head. "It's actually not that easy," he said. "Those are city keys, the kind you're not supposed to duplicate, right?"

"Yes," I replied. "I saw Josie's key, and I noticed how it had 'do not duplicate' stamped right on it."

"Which means the kiosk wouldn't have accepted it," my husband told me. "Those things are designed to reject any keys that aren't supposed to be duplicated. No, if Trent took the key, then he would have had to go to a not entirely scrupulous locksmith to get one made."

That little detail seemed to narrow the pool a

bit. "Do we have any unscrupulous locksmiths here in Globe?"

My husband's black brows pulled together. "Well, I don't like to pay attention to rumors, but I heard that Len Howard, one of the guys who works at the tire place down on Highway 60, has done some shady stuff like that. It's not super hard to get locksmith tools, so it's not impossible. The thing is, anything he might have done, he probably would have done it here in Globe, and that's not my jurisdiction. Henry would have a better idea of what the guy's been up to."

"If that's the case, I doubt Henry would want to talk to me about it," I said. "He's been pretty civil lately, but if I start poking around people who might not even be connected to Trent's murder at all, I can only imagine his reaction."

"Especially since Len runs with a rough crowd," Calvin remarked. "He's not the kind of guy I'd want my wife visiting unaccompanied."

Len Howard didn't sound like anyone I wanted to meet, either. But if there was even the slightest chance he might know something about how Trent had gotten into that supposedly locked gymnasium in the middle of the night, then I couldn't hold off from visiting him.

I smiled and told my husband, "Then I guess you'll have to come with me."

Dinner first, of course, which was fine considering I'd started making it a little after five and we were ready to sit down right around six. Calvin still wasn't overly thrilled with the idea of dropping into Globe's one and only dive bar, but better that than let me go by myself.

We petted a mystified Sadie goodbye, then got into his San Ramon tribal police SUV. Probably not the most inconspicuous ride in the world, but since almost everyone in Globe knew who Calvin was, trying to be incognito by driving my Renegade didn't make a lot of sense. Besides, I'd been running all over town that day and was only too happy to have him play chauffeur for a little while.

It felt odd to pull up in front of the bar, since it wasn't a place I'd ever visited, despite being located just a few blocks down the street from my shop and former apartment. Since it was only a little past seven and kind of early for people to start partying on a Friday night, the place wasn't too crowded, and I wondered if we should have waited until after eight or maybe even nine to come here.

But then Calvin leaned down and murmured in my ear, "At the end of the bar," and I realized this hadn't been a wild goose chase after all.

Sitting on a stool and nursing something that appeared to be whiskey on the rocks was a man I guessed must be in his middle or late fifties, with gray-streaked dark hair slicked back from a weathered face that looked like it had never heard of sunscreen. He stared down into the glass as though he was hoping to find the secrets of the universe within...or maybe just trying to discover a way to get out of the one he currently inhabited.

"Getcha something?" came a woman's voice, and I looked over to see woman around my age, maybe a year or so older, standing there and giving Calvin and me a curious look. She had dark blonde hair streaked with lighter platinum highlights, thick eyeliner, and pink gloss on lips that should have worn liner a few shades lighter than the one she sported at the moment.

Attached to her low-cut T-shirt—emblazoned with the bar's logo—was a small name tag that read "Amber."

Looked like we were about to kill two birds with one stone.

"Ginger ale," I said, since I didn't want to alienate her by refusing to order anything.

"Same for me," Calvin said in resigned tones.

Amber didn't quite roll her eyes, but I could tell she wasn't thrilled with our orders, even though there was an obvious reason why I wouldn't want to drink anything stronger than soda.

"You could've gotten a beer," I murmured, and my husband shook his head.

"We have a pact, remember?" he replied. "No alcohol touches these lips until it can touch yours. A deal's a deal."

I reached over and squeezed his hand. "Maybe we should go sit down by Len before someone else takes one of those seats."

There might not have been much risk of that—the bar wasn't anywhere close to crowded yet—but I knew it would look more suspicious if Calvin and I kept loitering near the doorway.

A brief nod, and then he led me to the barstools in question and helped me up on one of them before taking the stool closest to Mr. Howard. The older man's gaze might have flickered slightly as he took in his new bar companions, but he didn't say anything.

Right then, Amber came over with our two glasses of ginger ale. "Should I start a tab, or will this be it?"

"This is all, thanks," Calvin replied, and reached in his wallet so he could pull out a ten-dollar bill. "You can keep the change."

Although she'd been looking a little sulky about having to handle such a small tab, now she brightened as she realized we weren't quite the cheapskates she'd thought we were.

"Thanks," she said. "Holler if you need anything else."

I would...just as soon as I figured out a way to ask her if Nick Russell really had spent the night at her place the evening before.

In the meantime, though, we had Len Howard to worry about. Calvin swallowed some of his ginger ale, expression contemplative, which seemed to be my signal that I needed to follow his lead and allow the situation to develop naturally. I was sure Len knew exactly who my husband was, and initiating a conversation out of the blue would make it way too obvious that we'd come here only to talk to him.

To my surprise—and probably Calvin's as well—Len leaned toward my husband and said, "What do you want, Standingbear?"

A slight twitch of his mouth. "Was I that obvious?"

Len picked up his drink, swallowed some whiskey, and replied, "Well, I don't recall seeing you in here before, especially not with a pregnant wife in tow."

"I wanted to ask you something," I chimed in, since trying to act casual now appeared to be off the table.

"I'm sure you do," Len said, his tone almost musing. "Since your hobby is solving murders."

Clearly, my reputation had preceded me. "Did you make a key for Trent Reynolds last night?"

"I did."

Calvin and I exchanged a glance. I definitely hadn't been expecting Len Howard to come right out and admit he'd illegally duplicated a key the night before, but either he'd already consumed enough Crown Royal that he really didn't care, or he knew this wasn't Calvin's jurisdiction and there wasn't much my husband could do about the situation even if Len did spill some incriminating information.

Maybe it was a little of both.

"How did Trent even know to come to you for a key?" Calvin asked then. "It's not like he's a local."

Len inclined his head toward Amber, who was just stepping away from the bar with a big twenty-ounce glass of beer in either hand. "Amber told him."

That made sense, although I felt like we were still missing a few key details.

Luckily, Calvin was right on it.

"When did Trent meet Amber? I thought he just got into town yesterday."

"He did," Len said, although he made us wait a few seconds while he swallowed some more whiskey. "Yesterday afternoon, I guess. Sounds like he came in here to get a drink while he was waiting for his Airbnb to be ready. He talked to Amber, made it sound like he was some kind of big deal, invited her to that reception or whatever it was last night, and I guess at some point he texted her and said Josie was being a hard-ass about letting him back onto the site to do some setup and if Amber knew anyone who could help him out."

Well, now I knew why Amber Drummond had ended up at the reception. It sounded like Trent had cruised into town, spotted the Drift Inn as a likely spot to hang out while he was waiting for Mavis's cleaning crew to finish with his Airbnb, and then chatted up Amber and asked her to meet him at the reception that night. It sounded as if she'd gone there after she was off work, which was why she'd shown up so late. And clearly, she hadn't had any problem letting him know about Len, had probably hoped that doing so would earn her some brownie points.

What I couldn't quite understand was why she'd ended up going home with Nick when it was Trent who'd invited her to the reception...or maybe I did. It seemed as if Trent was much more interested in getting into the gym later that night and getting a leg up on the competition than having a booty call, whereas Nick had clearly been ready for a little something extra for his first night in Globe.

A lot more of the pieces were beginning to fit together now. At least I knew where Trent had obtained the key that had allowed him to sneak into the gym late last night after everyone was gone, although I still wasn't any closer to discovering who had slipped into the gym and drowned him in that vat of water. How had the killer even managed that? Had they knocked Trent out, filled the vat, and then coldly held his head under to finish the job?

Without any other evidence to contradict that theory, it sure felt like that must have been what happened.

"It's not a big deal," Len added, and sipped some more Crown Royal.

Personally, I thought it was, just because if Len hadn't duplicated that key for Trent, he wouldn't have been able to get into the gym, and therefore he probably wouldn't be dead. Since I doubted any jury in the world would convict Len of something like that, however, I had to settle for a noncommittal sound before I helped myself to some ginger ale. I never drank soda and it tasted way too sweet, but I knew I had to make an attempt to fit in.

"In the eyes of the law, probably not," Calvin said. "Misdemeanor kind of stuff. Still, giving Trent that key made him a prime target for whoever wanted him dead."

It seemed my husband's thoughts had run in the same channels as mine...not that such a realization surprised me too much. We were *simpatico* way more often than not.

Len gave a noncommittal lift of one shoulder and drank some more Crown Royal. I had to wonder how much he'd consumed tonight, and whether he'd driven or walked.

Hopefully, the latter.

Amber came by right then, empty-handed, and I figured I wasn't going to get a better opportunity than this. I slid off my barstool and went over to her.

"Excuse me."

She sent me a mildly curious glance. "Need another ginger ale after all?"

"No," I replied at once, since I knew I probably wouldn't even be able to get through the first one. "I wanted to ask you about Trent Reynolds."

Her eyes narrowed, almost obscuring the dark blue with the heavy false eyelashes she wore. "What a jerk. Goes and invites me to that reception, and then bails out as soon as he gets Len's info from me so he could go get that key made."

I had to agree that was something of a jerk move. To be honest, I hadn't been tracking all the brewers the entire time I was at the reception, so I hadn't even noticed how Trent must have disappeared partway through the event. "Is that what happened?"

"Basically." She paused there to reach up and

play with the silver cross she wore at her neck, then let out an annoyed breath. "I mean, I guess it worked out in the end because I ended up meeting Nick, but still."

It didn't work out for Trent, I thought, although I didn't bother to mention that pithy little detail to her. Clearly, everything was about Amber, and if Trent had met with foul play last night, then that was his fault for leaving her to fend for herself at the reception.

"Did Trent tell you why it was so important for him to get back into the gym last night?" I asked next, and Amber shifted her weight from one foot to the other, seeming to signal she already thought our conversation had gone on long enough.

"Said something about needing more time to set up his display," she replied, her tone one of extreme indifference. "It seemed kind of stupid to me. Anyway, I need to get back to work."

Before I could say anything to try to stop her, she'd turned back to the bartender, who'd already lined up several drinks on the counter for her. Since it really did look as though I was keeping her from taking care of her patrons, I didn't try to say anything else, and instead headed back to where Calvin was sipping his ginger ale and Len, having delivered all the information he felt necessary to reveal, was making serious inroads in his Crown Royal.

I tapped Calvin on the shoulder.

"Hey—let's get out of here."

My phone shrilled from the nightstand, and I sat bolt upright in bed, heart pounding, hand reaching for the damn thing so I could shut it off. I'd never heard it make that sound before, but—

Then my eyes focused on the home screen, and I realized why my phone had gone off like an air-raid siren.

That was the notification from my alarm system that something had gone terribly wrong at the shop.

Calvin was sitting up in bed as well, rubbing at his eyes. "Is that—"

"Yes," I said, knowing how curt I sounded. "It's the store security alarm."

"Hell."

No kidding. We both jumped out of bed and reached for the nearest clothing—in my case, the skirt and sweater and boots I'd been wearing the day before and had been too tired to put away when we got home from the Drift Inn. I'd slung the clothes over the side chair that sat a few feet away from the nightstand, and now I was damn glad I'd been so lazy.

My phone's screen kept flashing red, so I had to look at the alarm clock to see the time.

Three-fifteen.

Murmuring a silent apology to the baby in my belly for being woken up so rudely, I pulled on my clothes while Calvin also got dressed and ready to go. The alarm company I worked with had an armed response, but this was the first time I'd ever had the system go off, so I had no idea how fast they could get there.

I knew Calvin was going to burn rubber, though.

We were out the door in less than three minutes and roaring toward town on an empty highway, a tiny sliver of a moon hanging low in the sky in the west, almost like a faint beacon guiding us in.

"Why break into my store now?" I asked plaintively. "I mean, it's been there for years and I haven't had even a single attempt to rob the place."

"I'm hoping for a false alarm," Calvin replied, although I didn't think that scenario was very likely, considering we'd never had a problem like this before.

As we turned onto Bridge Street and sped toward the block where the shop was located, I could tell it hadn't been a false alarm at all. A white car with the security company's logo emblazoned on the door was parked out front, along with a

Globe P.D. police SUV. Since the police department headquarters were less than a block away, they probably could have walked, but maybe they'd come here from patrolling the streets in a different part of town.

But then my eyes focused on the storefront, and I realized the big picture window that gave the place so much charm—and was the focus of my seasonal decorations—had been smashed in, leaving a gaping dark hole behind.

I hurriedly unlocked the door and leaped out... well, waddled out...with Calvin close on my heels. As I approached the window, the man from the security company and the deputy talking to him paused to turn toward me.

"My phone told me something was up," I said, and the deputy—Colin Long—nodded. He was a fairly new addition to the force, a kid from Anthem who'd just graduated from college last summer.

"Looks like someone threw a rock through your window," he said, inclining his head toward the shattered storefront. Sure enough, a large chunk of gray stone, probably weighing at least four or five pounds, was sitting in the middle of the cheerful holiday display Hazel and I had put together only a few weeks earlier.

Seeing how it had pulverized the little group of Santa's elves that had been grouped with some books and incense holders brought tears to my eyes. Those poor little elves definitely hadn't deserved to get creamed like that.

"Any fingerprints?" Calvin said crisply.

Deputy Long straightened a little, as if he knew he was in the presence of a superior despite Calvin not having any real authority within Globe's town limits. "I haven't dusted it yet," he said, sounding apologetic. "I was talking to Mr. Stanton here, since he was first on the scene."

"Only by a few minutes," the man from the security company, who looked like he had a good thirty years on Deputy Long, said. "Tim Stanton, by the way. I got here as fast as I could, but whoever did this was long gone."

Which made it sound as though their intention had been to cause mayhem, and not to steal anything. True, I didn't keep the really valuable stuff in the store windows, just because I figured I shouldn't tempt fate, but the rock-thrower still could have scooped up some books and crystals if they'd been so inclined.

"We'll review the security footage, though," Tim Stanton continued. "There might be something in that. Let's go take a look."

Luckily, my tears had stayed in my eyes and hadn't flowed down my cheeks, so I hoped I looked relatively composed as I got the shop keys out of my purse and unlocked the door. A moment to reset the alarm—my hands shook more than I'd thought they would—but then we were all inside and heading back to the storeroom, where the hard drive that stored all the security footage was located.

Not that I had the place set up like Fort Knox or anything close to it. No, I had two cameras in the main shop space, one pointed toward the cash register and another toward the front window. It wasn't as though I had any surveillance outside— I'd thought it would be off-putting to my patrons to be filming them before they even walked in the door—so I just had to hope the one camera directed toward the front of the building might have captured something.

It had been so long since the security company rep had showed me how everything worked that I stepped aside to let Tim Stanton handle things. He worked the controls for the DVR expertly, bringing up the feed from the front camera and then jogging back to about ten minutes earlier.

"There he is," he said, quite unnecessarily, since I was pretty sure all of us could see the dark figure who approached the store, paused to get the rock out of their backpack, and then hurled it through the front window.

They'd obviously prepared for the eventuality of being filmed, because a black knitted cap was pulled down low, obscuring their hair and forehead, and a black scarf or muffler covered the lower half of their face. About all I could tell was that they seemed to be tall and broad-shouldered under the black puffer coat they wore and were most likely male. Otherwise, there were absolutely no clues as to the perpetrator's identity.

"Gloves," Calvin remarked, spying the dark fabric or possibly leather that covered the person's hands. "No point in dusting for fingerprints."

"They were prepared, that's for sure," Tim Stanton observed, while Deputy Long frowned.

"I'll take the rock into evidence anyway," he said. "Maybe the guy handled it before he put on the gloves. I'll also look around and see if there's any evidence of tire marks, that kind of thing."

It seemed like a long shot to me, but I knew the deputy was just trying to help. "Thank you," I said.

He headed out, and Tim Stanton turned back toward Calvin and me. "You can re-arm the alarm, but with the window like that...."

"It's all right," Calvin said, his tone grim. "I'll get some plywood and board it up until we can have someone come out here to give us an estimate on getting it fixed."

Which I guessed was going to cost a chunk of change, just because a big piece of sheet glass to fit in a vintage window frame measuring roughly five feet high and seven feet wide wasn't going to come cheap. The cost of replacing it wasn't what worried me, though. No—well, beyond the obvious anxiety over whether the rock-thrower was going to come back and finish the job—was the fear that we'd have to special-order the glass and I'd have to go through the entire holiday season with a big piece of plywood covering up my holiday displays.

"And I'll stay on guard here all night until you can get it handled," Tim said.

I wanted to protest that wasn't necessary, but I held my tongue. Ours was a quiet and mostly law-abiding town, and yet a gaping hole like that would be an obvious invitation for any less scrupulous types in the area to come inside and help them-selves to whatever they wanted.

"It won't take that long," Calvin promised.

And he was right. He called his brother Joe, explained the situation, and less than fifteen minutes later, Joe showed up with a big piece of plywood in the back of his truck and a nail gun. They had the window covered faster than I could have imagined, which meant there was no reason for Tim to hang around.

Or Deputy Long, who'd bagged the rock as promised and checked around the store, only to report that there didn't seem to be any obvious tire marks near the property, nor any other evidence to show the rock-thrower had been here at all.

Well, except for my shattered window.

Calvin thanked both men for their help,

adding, "And now I need to get my wife back to bed. We'll follow up in the morning."

They said they hoped we could get some sleep, and Calvin and I got back in his police-issue Durango. For a few moments, we were both quiet as we drove away.

Then I said in plaintive tones, "Who would do something like this?"

"I don't know," Calvin replied, night-dark eyes fixed on the equally dark road ahead of us.

"But I'm going to find out."

TEN

Lie Down With Dogs

IT WAS ALMOST FIVE BY THE TIME WE GOT
back to the house. My nerves were so frayed that I
doubted I'd be able to sleep a wink, but the baby
had other plans for me. Almost as soon as my head
hit the pillow, my eyes closed and I was down for
the count.

In fact, I slept so hard that I didn't wake up
until well past eight. Calvin came into the
bedroom, a cup of herbal tea in one hand.
"Thought you could use this," he said.

I took the tea from him, glad of its warmth
against my fingers. It reassured me that most things
were still normal, and even though I still was
shocked and scared and somehow violated, I had a
husband who loved me and a life that would go on
despite that one awful act of vandalism.

"Thank you," I said simply. "I really didn't expect to sleep in like this."

"You needed it," Calvin replied. "You were chasing around all over the place yesterday, and then to get woken up like that in the middle of the night—"

"Hazel!" I broke in, realizing she would be going to work at the shop in only an hour and a half.

"It's fine," Calvin said gently. "I just texted her and let her know what happened, and told her the shop would be closed today...and probably until we can get that window fixed."

Thank the Goddess for Calvin Standingbear. He always knew the exact right thing to do.

I sipped some of the tea. It seemed as if he'd let it sit a while before bringing it to me so it would be exactly the right temperature—warm enough to be soothing, but not so hot that I ran any risk of burning my tongue.

"How long have you been up?" I asked. Usually, I at least stirred when Calvin got out of bed, even on those occasions when I didn't have to be up for several more hours. Today, though, I seemed to have slept through a lot, because he was already dressed and showered, long black hair slicked back into its usual ponytail.

"About an hour," he replied. "Sadie wanted to

go out, so I let her outside and fed her, then went ahead and got showered. I was kind of expecting to hear something from the police, but then, it's Saturday."

"And we're dealing with a property crime, not a murder," I said, and sipped some more tea.

"Pretty much. I think once we got the plywood nailed up, they figured there wasn't much else to do." Calvin paused there. "We'll need to file a claim with your insurance."

I made a face. "What's the point?" I said. "They'll take forever to deal with the damage and jack up my rates into the bargain. I'll pay for it out of pocket."

Since Calvin knew how much I had in said "pocket," he didn't bother to argue with me. "Well, we can start calling around, then, and see who we can get out here to have that window repaired. I'm sure there must be someone in Phoenix who would be willing to come out here and take care of it."

Probably for an additional fee; most companies weren't thrilled about having to travel sixty or seventy miles for a single job. But while we had exactly one window company here in Globe, they were almost always swamped, and I knew I'd have to wait forever for them to take care of my shop's repairs.

"All right," I said. The whole mess with the

broken store window had almost made me forget about Trent Reynolds...but not quite. "Do you think we still need to have the forensic locksmith come out here now that we know how Trent got into the gym?"

Calvin sat down on the bed, but carefully, so he wouldn't jostle me or the drink I was holding. "I think it's still a good idea. Maybe Trent used a key, but how did the killer get into the building?"

"I just figured Trent forgot to lock the door behind him."

For a moment, Calvin considered my state-ment, but then he shook his head. "I'm not so sure about that," he replied. "Someone who went to the effort of obtaining a key illegally and then sneaking over there in the dead of night probably would have made sure the place was buttoned up so he wouldn't be disturbed."

That angle on the situation made sense. Also, since we'd actually found a locksmith willing to travel all the way out to Globe, I didn't think it would be very fair to cancel on him at the last minute. "Okay," I said before reaching over so I could set my cup of tea down on the coaster I always kept on my nightstand. "Sounds like I'd better take a shower, then."

Our appointment with the locksmith wasn't until noon, though, which meant I had time to answer a call from Josie asking me if I was all right. After assuring her that the shop had only suffered a broken window and nothing had been stolen—and that Calvin was working on finding a glazier who could come out ASAP—she said, "I just heard from a man named Scott Doyle. He says he's Trent's business partner and wants to go to the Airbnb to pick up his personal effects. It sounds like he's listed as Trent's emergency contact because Trent doesn't have any family in the area."

Although Trent Reynolds definitely hadn't been on my top ten list of favorite people on the planet, I couldn't help but experience a sad little pang at hearing Josie's words. It was hard to hear how alone Trent had been in the world.

I couldn't help wondering if he might have turned out a little differently if his parents hadn't died in that plane accident. Reading between the lines, it didn't seem as if his aunt had been very happy to take him in and had pushed him out of the house as soon as she legally could.

However, I couldn't change the past. All I could do now was try to find out who'd prevented Trent from having a future.

"When's Scott Doyle going over to the Airbnb?" I asked. Maybe talking to him wouldn't help me learn anything new about the case, but I always figured the more information, the better.

"You want to interview him?" Josie responded, her tone now almost eager. I got the impression she'd been holding back on pressuring me about the murder case because of what had happened to my shop the night before, but since it seemed as if Calvin and I had everything handled, she wanted me to get back to work.

"'Interview' might be too formal a word," I said. "I just thought it might help to get more insights about Trent from someone who knew him well."

Or at least, I had to assume that someone who was Trent's business partner—and who had been listed as his emergency contact—had to be privy to information none of his fellow competitors would possess.

"Scott told me he should be here a little after eleven," Josie said. "He's going to swing by Mavis's house to get a key. I can ask her to call me when he's leaving her place, and then I can text you so you can meet him at the Airbnb."

That sounded like a decent plan to me. There was always the chance that Scott would be in and out before I was able to intercept him, but I didn't think so. I could be at the vacation rental in about ten minutes, and it would take him longer than that to drive over there himself and then pack Trent's things.

"Perfect," I replied. "I'll be looking out for your text."

After I returned my phone to my purse, I went to the living room to find Calvin. He was sitting on the couch and petting Sadie, clearly happy to enjoy this rare quiet time in between handling business.

I told him about the plan Josie and I had concocted, and although my husband didn't appear completely happy to know I'd be setting out to meet another complete stranger, he only said, "Do you want me to come along?"

"Better not," I replied. "A lot of people are less chatty when they feel like they're being ganged up on."

"The two of us aren't exactly a gang," Calvin pointed out, and I smiled.

"True, but still, if it feels like a casual one-on-one conversation, I can usually get people to tell me a lot."

Because that had, in fact, happened on multiple occasions, he couldn't really argue with me.

"All right," he said. "Then I suppose we can meet at the gym at noon and see what the locksmith has to say."

I told him that sounded like a good idea. At the

same time, though, I couldn't help worrying about how quickly time was passing. Even if the locksmith discovered that the locks at the gym had in fact been picked, I didn't know how much closer such a finding would get us to tracking down the killer.

And the brewers were supposed to be arriving at the gym to finish their setup at four, with the event itself starting at five.

Five hours to get all this sorted out.

I tried to tell myself a lot could happen in that stretch of time. After all, I now knew that Trent had gone to Len Howard to get the key made that gave him access to the gym, and I knew Nick Russell's alibi was solid because he'd been at Amber Drummond's house all night. The other contestants also had alibis, in my mind, although I had to admit seeing auras that revealed a person's good character weren't the sort of thing any judge would allow...or most juries would accept.

Well, I could stew and fret about it, or I could put on my big girl panties and go over and talk to Scott Doyle about Trent Reynolds.

I decided to do the latter.

However, since I had a little time to kill, I decided to break out my Tarot cards and see if they were willing to offer a little extra illumination on the situation. This strategy only seemed to work about half the time, since I often got the feeling that the cards thought they'd told me what I needed to know and it was up to me to puzzle out the meaning of the cards I'd pulled.

This seemed to be the case today, because after a couple of shuffles and getting nothing more than what I fondly referred to as "minor arcana mish-mash," I knew I was on my own here. The thought crossed my mind to reach out to Grandma Ellen to see if she had any pearls of wisdom to impart, but since I'd spoken to her less than three weeks ago while dealing with that whole Melanie Knowles nightmare, I had a feeling my grandmother would be less than eager to help me out with my current conundrum. That particular case had directly involved me and my friends, while Trent Reynolds' death, although tragic and a serious P.R. problem for Josie, wasn't anything that affected me too directly. I'd probably go to all the trouble of summoning Grandma Ellen's spirit for advice, only to have her tell me I needed to work this one through on my own.

Before I could get too annoyed by the whole situation, though, my phone pinged.

Scott's on his way to the Airbnb.

Saved by the bell. I grabbed my purse, threw on a jacket, and hurried out to the garage. Calvin had left a while earlier, saying he needed to do a few things at the San Ramon police building before he headed over to Globe. I felt a little bad about that, just because I knew he'd been scheduled to work today and had jiggered things around so he'd be available to meet the locksmith and also accompany me to the brewing competition later this afternoon. Even if I wasn't able to solve this murder in time, I wanted my husband and me to be there for Josie to show our support.

When I pulled up to the attractive Spanish-style house where Trent had been staying, I noticed a big white Ram truck parked out front, presumably Scott Doyle's vehicle. In fact, right after I got out of my Renegade and headed up the walk, the front door of the house opened, and a man probably seven or eight years older than I emerged. He had a duffle bag in one hand and what looked like a laptop carrier in the other, and seemed a little startled to see me approach.

"Can I help you?" he asked.

"I hope so," I said. "My name's Selena—I'm a friend of Josie's."

His gaze slid to my thickened midsection for just a fraction of a second. He was only a few inches taller than I, stocky rather than chubby, with wavy dark hair and brown eyes. "I hope she didn't send you over here to help get Trent's stuff out of the house. There really isn't that much."

"Oh, that's not why I'm here," I replied. "I wanted to talk to you about Trent."

Something in his stance became instantly wary. "Like what?"

No point in beating around the bush, I supposed. "I'm helping Josie figure out who killed Trent. I was hoping you might be able to give me some details that would help me fill in the blanks as to who might have had a motive."

Scott Doyle didn't exactly relax, but something in the way his expression became almost resigned told me he wasn't going to send me packing. "Okay. Just let me put this stuff in my truck, and then we can talk. Door's open—go on in and have a seat."

Inwardly rejoicing that he hadn't told me to get lost, I went inside and sat down on the cream linen sofa. A minute later, Scott came in as well, and pulled up the armchair set off to one side.

"I assume you've already been poking around a bit," he said, his tone almost wry.

"A little," I admitted. Sticking with the whole truthfulness thing, I added, "Did you know about the accusations against Trent?"

"For stealing other people's formulas?" Scott responded, then went on without waiting for my reply, "Yeah, I did. Kind of had to, since the lawsuit Elijah Wright filed was against our LLC, not Trent personally."

Ouch. That must have been fun. Had the process server delivered the papers at one of Trent's brewhouses?

Since that particular detail wasn't exactly relevant to my current line of questioning, I decided to leave it aside for now. "Did you think the suit had any merit?"

Now Scott's gaze slid away from mine, as though he really didn't want to answer my question. But since his business partner was now dead, I supposed he'd decided it really didn't matter if he talked some trash about Trent now.

"At first, no," Scott said. "Then I did some asking around, and I found out Trent kind of had a reputation for that sort of thing. My fault for not investigating him more closely, I guess."

I tried hard not to sound judge-y, but I wasn't sure how well I succeeded. "You went into business with him without doing any research?"

A sheepish shrug, and Scott replied, "He seemed like a decent guy. I went to his brewpub in Glendale all the time, and we started talking about stuff. He told me he wanted to expand but was having a hard time getting the capital lined up, and I said I'd been interested in investing in a restaurant for a while and wanted to help out. That's how he was able to open a second place in Fountain Hills, and then another in Tempe."

Not being an expert in restaurant management, I had no idea how much it would have cost to expand into two more locations. A decent chunk, I guessed. It also begged the question as to why Trent needed an investor when he'd supposedly inherited a bunch of money from his parents' estate.

I went ahead and asked about that, and Scott only shook his head.

"He said a lot of his liquid capital was tied up in other investments, and also that he wanted a business partner so he'd have someone to bounce ideas off of. It seemed like a reasonable explanation at the time."

"But it wasn't?"

"No," Scott said. He'd been pretty forthright so far, but I could tell from the way he shifted in his seat and his eyes wouldn't quite meet mine from time to time that he was uncomfortable talking about the subject. "I got played, I guess. Turned out Trent liked to spend money...like, a lot of money. A few months ago, he went out and bought one of those Wrangler Gladiators, you know, the things that look like a Jeep but with a truck bed?"

I nodded because I knew exactly the kind of vehicle he was talking about. Calvin and I had passed by several Gladiators when we went to buy my much more modest Renegade, so I knew a tricked-out version of the big truck-style Jeep could cost nearly a hundred grand, which seemed absolutely nuts to me. Not that I didn't know people spent all kinds of crazy money on cars, but just that I couldn't really justify paying so much. Maybe for a Maserati or something, but not a Jeep.

"He didn't have the money for that kind of thing," Scott went on. "He also already had a perfectly good truck. But he was like that—he never worried about whether something was a good idea or not, just went ahead with it if it was something he wanted."

"If he didn't have the money up front, how did he pay for the Jeep?" I asked.

Now Scott looked distinctly uncomfortable. "He did favors for people, and they paid him good money for it."

"What kind of favors?"

Scott rubbed his hands on the knees of his jeans, and I thought I saw a gleam of sweat on his brow even though the room was almost chilly, the heat probably turned down to the mid-sixties when Trent departed to go to the gym in the dead of night and then left there because no one had been here to adjust it back to a more comfortable level.

A little shiver worked its way down my back as I thought of all the things left undone when a life was suddenly cut short.

"You're not going to tell anyone this, are you?"

I wished I could say no, but if Scott confessed a

piece of actual criminality, I might have to go to Henry with it.

Or maybe not. Surely whatever Scott had to reveal had to do with Trent and their businesses in the Phoenix area, and therefore would be something way out of Henry Lewis's jurisdiction.

"Hopefully not," I replied, which was about the only assurance I could give. "But if it's something that could lead to Trent's murderer, then I might have to go to the authorities with it."

Scott shifted in his chair again, one hand reaching up to ruffle the hair at the back of his head. Because it was naturally wavy, it now looked more mussed than ever.

"We were in the process of building a new brewpub out in Goodyear," he said. "It seemed to be nothing but problems—delays on materials, issues with the inspections, that kind of stuff. Trent was handling the whole project, though, so I didn't have all the details. But then I found out the real reason why we weren't going to be opening any time soon."

"And what was that?" I inquired. All the issues he'd just related to me didn't seem terribly unusual, although I knew they must have been frustrating.

Now Scott rubbed both his palms against the knees of his jeans, as though doing so could somehow absolve him from being involved in what he was about to relate.

In an undertone, the words coming out fast, he said, "Trent found some guy who was paying him a lot of money to make fentanyl in the unfinished restaurant. The kitchen was done—it was the bar and the seating areas that hadn't been completed yet. The guy gave him a cut of the sales for allowing them to use the kitchen to make drugs."

Of all the explanations I'd been expecting, I had to admit that was the last one I'd thought I'd hear. After giving him a startled blink, I said, "Did you go to the police?"

Looking shamefaced, Scott replied, "I was afraid to. I mean, these people Trent was dealing with aren't the kind of people you want to cross, you know?"

I did. Or rather, while I didn't have any personal experience with drug dealers, I had to believe they'd take a dim view of anyone who would reveal their identities to the authorities.

"Do you think they're the ones who killed Trent?" I asked next. After all, pissed-off drug dealers sure seemed like plausible murder suspects to me.

"I don't know," Scott said. "I mean, I could tell he was worried about something, but he wouldn't tell me what it was. He just said he was going to enter this competition, and that would fix everything."

True, Josie was offering ten grand in prize

money, but that seemed like a drop in the bucket compared to the kind of cash Trent had apparently been throwing around. Had he been counting on winning and parlaying that good publicity into more backers, more people to invest in his operation?

Possibly. Without him around to ask, it was really hard to know for sure.

"I'm sorry you had to deal with all this," I said, and Scott blinked at me, as if surprised that a stranger might show compassion to someone who'd clearly gotten himself into something much more problematic than he'd planned.

Looking down at his hands, which rested on his knees, he replied, "Thanks. It's my own fault, though. I should've done more checking to see whether Trent was really on the up and up."

I somehow doubted Trent would have included his arrangement with a bunch of drug dealers on his balance sheet. Rather than point that out, though, I only said, "What happens now? With your company's holdings, I mean."

Scott shrugged. "Well, Trent was the driving force behind the brewpubs, so I guess I'll have to see if anyone's willing to buy them. The one in Goodyear...I don't know. I have to hope that Trent's deal died with him, and the drug guys won't have an issue with me selling that one, too. It's in a decent location and they could use some more bars and restaurants in the area, so maybe I won't take a complete bath on it."

"You should probably go to the police about the fentanyl dealers," I said gently, but Scott immediately shook his head.

"And have them come after me, too?" he responded. "No way. The only thing I can do now is hope they'll go away and find someone else to give them space for their operation. I'm done with all of this."

He stood up then and I rose as well, guessing this was his way of telling me our conversation was over. Which was fine—he'd probably already confessed a lot more than he was planning to.

We went to the door, and I paused there. Maybe I shouldn't ask the question, but my curiosity got the better of me.

"Where'd you get the money to invest in Trent's operation, anyway?"

An ironic smile pulled at Scott's lips. "I invested in bitcoin back when it was worth nothing and sat on it. Pretty easy way to make ten million bucks."

Even easier than having a half-crazy L.A. necromancer leave it to you in his will. "I hope you didn't invest it all in Trent's brewpubs," I said.

"Oh, I'm not *that* stupid," Scott replied. "But still, losing a million or so over something like this definitely stings. You have a good day, Selena."

I nodded and headed out, thoughts racing.

Had the fentanyl dealers killed Trent because he was about to renege on their deal, or because he owed them money? It all seemed plausible enough, and yet...

...and yet, I still didn't know whether that was the actual truth of the matter.

ELEVEN

Slippery Subjects

CALVIN, WHO WAS WAITING AT THE GYM when I showed up a few minutes after my talk with Scott Doyle, looked less than pleased after I related my story.

"It was probably the drug dealers," he said. "They don't tend to worry too much about knocking a piece off the chessboard if it stops being useful."

Maybe so. I'd never watched *Breaking Bad* or any other shows in that vein, so I wasn't exactly keyed into the behavior of drug dealers and their code of honor, such as it was. "I'm not sure," I said, and immediately, Calvin gave me a keen look.

"A feeling?" he asked, and I nodded.

"I know it would be easy to pin this on those less-than-savory characters Trent was doing business with," I said. "But I don't know. It feels too easy."

Calvin let out a breath. "Okay. I'll go with your gut on this one because it's been right too many times before now. All the same, I think it's a good idea to call the local police department's tip line and let them know something pretty underhanded has been going on at the brewpub under construction in their town."

I had to agree with my husband on that one. It was possible the fentanyl dealers had cleared out as soon as they learned Trent was dead, but if not, then there was still a chance to catch them red-handed.

Calvin got out his phone, searched around a bit, and made the call. He didn't identify himself, only said he had good reason to believe a restaurant currently under construction in their town was hosting fentanyl-cooking parties in its kitchen, and then touched the screen to end the call.

"Hopefully, they'll take it seriously and won't think it's a prank."

"No one would ever think someone with your voice was pulling a prank," I replied, and Calvin just shook his head. He did have a nice, deep, velvety voice, not the sort of voice that would belong to some high school kid who thought it might be fun to call in crank calls to the local police department.

"Well, we'll see. But at least now I feel like I've done my due diligence."

We'd been standing in the parking lot and talking, bundled up against the clear, chilly day, and just as Calvin finished speaking, a white van with a padlock logo painted on the side and the words "SpeedyLock" emblazoned under it pulled up and parked nearby. An older gentleman, maybe in his early or mid-sixties, gray hair ruffled by the brisk breeze, climbed out of the driver's-side door.

"Calvin?" the man ventured, and my husband nodded as we took a few steps toward the newcomer. "I'm Ed Fellowes—we talked on the phone yesterday."

"Hello, Ed," my husband replied. "Yes, I'm Calvin, and this is my wife Selena. Let me show you the locks we're interested in."

Ed nodded. "Just let me get out my tools."

Calvin and I waited while he grabbed a toolbox from the rear of the van, and then the three of us headed over to the main door that led into the gymnasium. At once, Ed got out a small penlight and several screwdrivers and proceeded to dismantle the lock so he could inspect the interior. During this procedure, neither Calvin nor I said anything, hardly wanting to breathe so we wouldn't disturb Ed at his work.

But then he shook his head, even as his nimble fingers began to put the lock back together. "I couldn't find any evidence of tampering," he said. "The lock's old and could stand to be replaced, but it still doesn't have the kind of scratches I'm looking for."

Calvin sent me a searching look from under his eyebrows, but I refused to be dissuaded this early in the game. "There's another door that leads into the kitchen," I said. "Why don't you take a look at that one?"

"Show me," Ed replied.

He gathered up his toolbox, and we went around a corner of the building to the kitchen door. This side of the gym was much less protected from the wind, and I found myself shivering despite the heavy wool wrap I'd thrown around my shoulders as I left the house earlier.

Even though he was from the Phoenix area—which often was a good fifteen to even twenty degrees warmer than Globe—Ed didn't seem to pay much attention to the wind's bite. No, he settled down to work on the lock just like he had the one on the main door, carefully disassembling it, shining his penlight into the parts he'd laid down on a soft white cloth so he wouldn't lose track of any of them.

"Nothing on this one, either," he said, and I frowned.

"So, no one picked the locks to get into the building," Calvin said, and Ed gave a small shake of his head before beginning to put the lock back together.

"Not that I can tell," he replied, then returned his attention to the metal bits and pieces on the cloth in front of him. "But," he went on as he slipped the reassembled lock back into its place in the door, "this one is in even worse shape than the one out front. It doesn't always catch. See?"

And he opened the door and went inside. From outside, we could hear the sound of the dead-bolt being clicked into place.

"Try opening it," Ed said next, voice muffled slightly by the door, and I reached out a hand and was able to lift the latch without any problem, revealing him standing in the opening.

"But I heard you lock it," I protested.

He smiled, showing teeth that were strong and straight and just a little bit yellow. "That's what I mean. It feels like the deadbolt is falling into place, but because the tumblers are worn, it slips. That means pretty much anyone could get in here even without a key."

No wonder there hadn't been any sign of forced entry. Trent had let himself in with a key he probably hadn't needed in the first place, and the killer—whether a drug dealer from Goodyear or someone else—had simply let himself in without any trouble at all.

They hadn't left fingerprints, either, since I

knew Henry and his team had checked on that while they were conducting their investigation. Or rather, there were fingerprints, a muddle of evidence left behind by Josie and the custodial staff and half the people competing in the brewing contest. However, I didn't think the police had found anything that wasn't easily explained.

"Thanks, Ed," Calvin said. If he was at all disappointed by the lack of useful evidence turned up by having the forensic locksmith drive all the way to Globe, he didn't show it. "And thanks again for coming out here on a Saturday."

"It's fine," Ed replied as he returned his tools to their box. "I'll still get home in time to watch the big game."

My husband smiled, even as I inwardly thanked the universe—not for the first time—that he wasn't a big fan of team sports. Every once in a while he'd turn on a game, more to stay at least slightly informed so he could talk about it with one of his brothers, but otherwise, he could take it or leave it. And while I was the last person to ever deny someone their hobbies, I had to admit I was definitely not a sports fan and glad that I didn't have to worry about being a football widow.

We walked Ed back to his truck, then waved as he pulled out of the old high school's parking lot and headed back to the highway. There hadn't been any mention of payment, telling me Calvin had probably handled that earlier when he was setting up this appointment.

"Well, what now?" I asked, knowing frustration had leaked into my voice despite my best efforts to keep it out.

"Go home and regroup," my husband replied. Reaching over to take my hand and give it a gentle squeeze, he added, "We actually learned something useful today. Despite what the TV shows might want you to think, there aren't that many people out there who can successfully pick a lock. Now that I know the lock on the kitchen door is faulty, it makes a lot more sense that the murderer was able to get into the building without anyone noticing."

All right, I'd admit it was an interesting data point. Whether I believed it was truly useful the way Calvin did...well, I wasn't quite ready to go there yet.

"Okay," I said. "Let's get out of here."

We spent some time calling around to glaziers in the Phoenix area—well, the ones that were open on a Saturday, anyway. To my infinite relief, we were able to find someone who could come out on Monday afternoon to measure the broken store window and order the glass. They made it sound as if it would probably take a few days after that to come back with the new pane and install it, but at least now I knew we wouldn't have to worry about weeks going past with that piece of plywood marring the façade of my cute little shop.

The whole time, though, my gaze kept moving to the clock on the mantel in the living room, how the seconds and minutes and hours kept moving past, relentless, unforgiving. Calvin and I might have added a few extra pieces to the puzzle, but they still weren't enough to make it anything close to whole.

A little after three, however, my phone rang. Calvin had gone out for a bit to help one of his brothers move a new big-screen TV into his living room—an early present from Aaron's wife, so he'd be able to watch all the Christmas Day games in wide-screen splendor—so at first I thought it must be him calling me to let me know he was going to be a little later coming home than he'd planned.

But no, it was Josie.

At once, I grabbed the phone and put it up to my ear. I'd thought she must be hip-deep in getting ready for the brewing contest, since it was scheduled to start in less than two hours, but maybe she had some news for me.

In fact, that's exactly what she had.

"They arrested someone!" she exclaimed, so exuberantly that I had to hold my phone away from my ear to lower the risk of damage to my eardrum.

"They, who?" I asked.

She made an impatient noise. "The Goodyear police. Henry just contacted me to let me know they'd called him to tell him someone had left an anonymous tip about a fentanyl lab in the area, and they arrested two suspects, one of whom they're charging with Trent Reynolds' murder."

My head was spinning a bit. Yes, of course I'd hoped that Calvin's call about the makeshift meth lab in the brewpub would yield some fruit, but I hadn't thought things would progress so quickly. "Do you know why they charged the one suspect with Trent's murder?"

"Henry didn't go into a lot of details," Josie replied. "He just told me the person charged with murder has a lot of priors, and I guess he confessed that Trent owed him hundreds of thousands of dollars. That sounds like grounds enough for me."

To most people, it probably would. However, I couldn't quite ignore the little niggle at the back of my mind that told me the Goodyear police had arrested the wrong man. Or rather, while the person currently in custody probably had lots of reasons to be arrested—such as running a drug lab and probably a street team as well to distribute the deadly goods they produced—some deep instinct kept whispering that their suspect wasn't a murderer.

Or at least, not the murderer in this particular case.

But I wouldn't say any of that to Josie, of course. She was obviously elated that she'd been granted an eleventh-hour reprieve, and that the investigation into Trent Reynolds' murder had been tied up with a neat little bow. Now she could go ahead with the contest without having to worry that the killer might still be lurking around somewhere.

I, on the other hand....

"That's great news," I replied, then added, "Do you have any extra tickets? I think Calvin and I might like to attend after all."

"For you? Definitely," she said at once, sounding cheered up that I'd changed my mind about coming to the brewing contest. I'd begged off because neither Calvin nor I were all that into beer, and even if we were, I couldn't exactly be tasting the competitors' wares in my current condition.

Now, though...now something was telling me I needed to be there, that the police hadn't caught the right person and the suspect was still out there somewhere. My instincts might have steered me wrong from time to time, but I'd still learned I shouldn't ignore them.

"I'll have the tickets waiting for you at the door," Josie told me. "I'm so glad you decided to come after all."

"Wouldn't miss it," I responded, and she ended the call there, telling me she had a million things to do.

I doubted that was hyperbole, either. In a very short amount of time, the High Country Brewing Competition would be throwing open its doors.

As to what might happen beyond those doors...

...well, I supposed I'd find out soon enough.

TWELVE

Pick a Winner

"Why the sudden change of heart?" Calvin asked when I called him at his brother's house after my call from Josie ended.

"Because I just don't think the Goodyear police have the right person," I replied. "Something's telling me I need to be at the contest and see how all the participants interact with each other. Maybe if I'm there, I'll find a clue that leads to the real killer."

A brief silence. The Goddess only knew I'd asked Calvin for a lot of things over the years, but I didn't think this a huge request, especially since he'd already planned to be home before the competition got up a good head of steam.

"Okay," he said. "We're almost done mounting the TV, anyway. Give me about fifteen more minutes."

"No problem," I chirped, glad I hadn't needed to put too much pressure on him. Being a nag really wasn't my style, but I also didn't want to miss out on whatever might be going on at the brewing contest.

Those fifteen minutes would give me extra time to get ready.

I didn't go crazy, of course, but I did put on a cheerful sweater dress whose Nordic pattern somehow managed to minimize my baby bump rather than make it look twice as large as it already was, brushed my hair, and freshened my makeup. Sadie watched these preparations with a wary look in her big brown eyes, as if she knew all too well that her mistress primping for something meant she was going to be left alone at the house in the very near future.

Calvin came home, gave me a kiss, and said, "Guess I'd better change."

"It's not a fancy event," I told him, but he just shook his head.

"No, these clothes aren't fit for going to any kind of public event. Just give me a minute."

Rather than argue, I pressed a kiss against his cheek and said, "sure," mostly because he was right. Since the only things we'd thought we had on the docket today were meeting with the locksmith and Calvin's quick trip to his brother's house to install the TV, he was wearing his oldest, rattiest jeans and a black sweatshirt that had gone through the wash too many times and had faded to a dingy gray.

While I waited, I turned on the TV to see if there was anything on the news about the arrests in Goodyear. Unfortunately, there was no local news to be had, just cable stuff that I doubted would be reporting on the arrest of a drug dealer in the greater Phoenix area, even one who'd been accused of murder. No, I'd just have to try to catch the ten o'clock news after dinner tonight.

Calvin emerged from the bedroom, still casual in jeans and boots and a zip-up fleece pullover, but much more socially acceptable because those items were newer. "Do I pass muster?" he asked.

"You know you do," I said, and went over and wrapped my arms around his waist. It wasn't quite as easy to snuggle up against him as it had been before my pregnancy, but I was still able to get my arms all the way around him...barely. "You clean up real good, Calvin Standingbear."

He grinned and pressed a kiss against the top of my head. "So do you, Selena Marx."

I smiled back at him, and, hand in hand, we headed out the door—well, after I bent down to pat Sadie on the head and tell her we wouldn't be too late. The schedule for the contest involved tasting by the judges from five to around six-thirty or so and then some kind of beer garden get-together afterward, but obviously Calvin and I wouldn't be sticking around for that. No, we'd come home and have a quiet dinner, and talk about what we'd seen at the competition.

Time to find out if my instincts were right... and that the killer was still out there somewhere.

As Josie had promised, we had a set of two-day passes waiting for us at the door. I didn't know for sure whether we'd need to attend both days, but it had been thoughtful of her to supply us with those, just in case.

And I had to admit I was a little surprised by how crowded the venue was. As far as I could tell, my friend's worries that a lot of people would decide not to come had been completely unfounded.

Had word of the supposed murderer's arrest already made the rounds?

Hard to say.

We entered the gym, which felt much more festive now than the last time I'd been here, with people milling around and holiday music blaring from speakers placed at strategic intervals around the space. I'd already seen the fancy booths intended for the competitors, but I hadn't been expecting the small marketplace that had been set up on one side of the gym or the small food court that looked as if it was carrying wares from several of our local food trucks.

No wonder Josie had told me she had a million things to do.

Calvin and I had only taken a few short steps before I heard Hazel calling my name. We paused as she approached us, looking both pleased and a little confused.

"I thought you weren't coming today," she said. "And especially now that someone's been arrested for Trent Reynolds' death."

News definitely traveled fast around here. But then, Hazel's husband Chuck was one of the three judges, and I supposed Josie would have let them know what was going on.

"There's been an arrest," I replied. "But I'm not sure they've got the right person."

"Your cards told you that?" Hazel asked. She didn't sound completely skeptical—she'd seen me turn out to be right about these sorts of things more often than not—but at the same time, she tended to be a very practical person despite her artistic nature, and I knew sometimes she had a hard time believing all this woo-woo stuff was actually effective.

"Not my cards," I said. "Just a feeling. Anyway,

I thought it couldn't hurt to swing by and spend a little time here, see if I pick up on anything."

Calvin glanced around the space. "Has the judging started yet?"

"No," Hazel replied. "About five more minutes, I think. They're going to do the lagers and wheat beers and pilsners today, and then tomorrow it'll be the heavier stuff."

Like Elijah Wright's Chile Whisperer IPA, I thought.

But no, Josie had said everyone was entering new brews at this competition, so it wouldn't be anything that anyone had tasted before, and nothing Trent would have been able to steal.

"Chuck's already at the judges' table, though," she went on. "Why don't we go on over so you can say hi?"

This sounded like a good idea to me. My instincts had guided me here but hadn't told me exactly what I was supposed to be looking for, which meant my best bet was probably to go with the flow and see what turned up.

As promised, Chuck was sitting at the judges' table, along with Henry Lewis and Brett Woodrow, Josie's nephew. She was nowhere to be found, and I assumed she must be putting out a fire somewhere. I had to admit it felt a little strange to see Henry sitting there in a plaid shirt and sweater and not his usual working uniform of a jacket and white shirt and tie. Almost all of our interactions were of the sort where he was acting in his official capacity, although Calvin and I bumped into him and his wife Joyce at the local Walmart from time to time.

We all exchanged greetings. Chuck's expression was one of vague surprise, since he, too, had thought Calvin and I were going to sit this one out. After Hazel sent him a sideways glance, though he seemed to pick up that he shouldn't ask any awkward questions.

"Nice to see you here," he said, while Henry only lifted an eyebrow.

"This doesn't seem like your cuppa, Selena," he remarked. "Especially now."

"Oh, we're just here to support Josie," I said airily. "We figured we'd wander a bit, watch some of the judging, and then head on home. It looks like she's got a great crowd here, though."

"She does," the police chief agreed. "I guess a simple thing like murder isn't enough to scare people away from a beer garden."

In the seat next to him, Brett grinned. He was a few years older than Calvin, not overly tall, but wiry and stronger than he looked. Good thing, too, since he'd come to my rescue more than once over the past couple of years when I'd run afoul of a suspect who figured the easiest way to escape murder charges was to make sure I was out of commission...permanently. He added, "Or maybe it's fear of what my aunt would do if they didn't show up to one of her events."

This remark was more hyperbole than anything else—I had a feeling most of the people in attendance didn't even know who Josie was—but then again, I never wanted to underestimate how much influence Josie Woodrow had on others.

We all chuckled a little, and before Henry could ask any more probing questions as to why Calvin and I had suddenly decided to show up at the competition, I said I wanted to take a look at the craft fair on the other side of the room.

Hazel opted to stay in the judging area—and promised she'd save seats for Calvin and me—and we walked away. Not too fast, though, nothing to make Henry Lewis think I was in a hurry to leave.

Calvin, of course, wasn't fooled for a second. "You really didn't want Henry picking your brain, did you?"

"No, I didn't," I replied. We were already in the craft area, since it wasn't too far from the judges' table, so I picked up a handmade bowl and pretended to admire its beautifully fired reactive glaze. Actually, I wasn't pretending all that much; the bowl was gorgeous, and I fully intended to take it home with me. "I don't want him ascribing any ulterior motives to our presence here."

"Even if we're oozing with them," Calvin remarked with a grin.

"Even if," I said, refusing to let him get to me. "Are you okay with carrying this bowl around? Because I want to buy it."

"I think I can handle that," he said, still smiling.

True, it wasn't a very big bowl, only about six inches across. I handed it to the woman running the booth, along with a couple of twenties. Once the bowl was safely wrapped up and placed in a bag, I gave it to Calvin.

"Okay, now it looks as if we were just here to shop," I told him. "Let's wander a little and then head back to the judges' table."

Expression amused, he said, "Lead on, Ms. Tour Guide."

I wrinkled my nose at him and then did a quick pass of the rest of the booths. Several of them were selling T-shirts, which had never been my thing even before I would have had to stretch them across my pregnant belly, and several more had all kinds of beer paraphernalia to offer. None of that was of much interest to me, either, but I still did my best to look interested as we glanced at the various wares before beginning to wend our way back to the judges' table.

The whole time, though, I hadn't seen any of the remaining contestants, and I began to wonder if coming here had been such a good idea after all.

My feet were starting to hurt, and a large part of me wanted to pack it in and go home.

That would be way too obvious, however, so we found Hazel in one of the rows of seats arranged in front of the judges' table and settled ourselves down next to her.

"Find anything interesting?" she asked.

"I got a gorgeous bowl," I replied.

She nodded, expression almost contemplative. "I've been thinking about trying pottery lately. We've got a shed on the property that Chuck said I could convert to a studio if I wanted to."

"I never knew you were into pottery," I said, and Hazel shrugged.

"I took a few classes in college, but I knew painting was more my thing. Still, it would be fun to play with when I want to take a break from my canvases."

"Especially since you've already got a place to work," I commented. The ranch Chuck had inherited from his parents was large, more than three hundred acres, with a six-bedroom house and several outbuildings. One room had already been turned into Hazel's art studio, but I could see why Chuck might want a pastime as messy as pottery done somewhere other than the main house. I loved how he supported her in all her various endeavors, though, and was quietly proud of the way she'd been gaining more recognition and having more gallery shows. Some people might have said they were an odd sort of couple, the all-American football star rancher and the quirky artist, but I knew their rough edges and angles suited one another perfectly, just as Calvin's and mine did as well.

However, I stopped there when I realized Josie had stepped out in front of the judge's table, all bright smiles and equally bright red and green plaid jacket. I had to wonder where she got all her holiday-themed clothes, since she seemed to have a different outfit for almost every occasion.

"Thank you so much for coming here," she said. Her voice was amplified to carry over the crowd, and I realized she had a small mic pinned to the lapel of her jacket. "While we had tragedies and complications to overcome, I'm very happy to announce that the judging will continue as planned, and also that poor Trent Reynolds' killer is already in custody. Let's honor his memory by having the best High Country Brewing Competition ever!"

That didn't seem too hard to me, considering this was the first one ever held, but I didn't say anything, of course. Next to me, Calvin shifted in his seat but otherwise didn't show any outward response to her words, although I had a feeling he was thinking much the same thing.

The people gathered to watch the judging

clapped, though, and a few of them murmured to one another. Expressing surprise that the murderer was already in custody? Hard for me to say, since I couldn't really hear their individual words, only that they'd responded in some way to her announcement.

Having gotten that piece of business out of the way, she went on, "And now, let me announce our judges. While not professional beer-makers, they do have a keen appreciation for the brewmaster's arts. Chuck Langdon!"

He half stood from his chair, looking vaguely embarrassed. People clapped, and I noticed how some of the women in the audience sent him admiring glances, possibly a little surprised that one of the judges would be such obvious man-candy. After a second or two, though, he sat back down again, looking as if he was rethinking his decision to agree to be a judge in the first place.

After that, Josie introduced Henry Lewis and Brett Woodrow. The clapping was a little more sporadic but still polite, although I could tell people were hoping Josie would move on to the meat of today's business.

She seemed to pick up on the vibe, because she said briskly, "Today's judging will encompass lagers, pilsners, and wheat beers. Tasting is blind, of course. The judges will take notes, confer after each round, and determine a first and second place in each category."

I wondered why there wasn't a third place, then realized when you only had five competitors over-all, anything below second would start to feel a lot like a participation trophy.

The crowd fell quiet as two women in their early twenties who I guessed had been recruited from the local community college came out with trays filled with small half-pint glasses partway filled with beer. Each of the glasses had a number on it—corresponding to a number assigned to each beer-maker by Josie, I assumed. They placed the glasses in front of the judges, then retreated to the sidelines, their trays now tucked under their arms.

"The lagers," Josie intoned, and each of the judges picked up their first glass of beer, sipped, and sipped again.

Clearly, they'd been instructed not to drain the glasses, probably a good idea considering how much beer they were going to have to consume over the course of the next hour. A pause while they all took notes, drank some water to clear their palates, and then it was time to move on to the pilsners.

This all took longer than I'd thought it would, a good ten or fifteen minutes for each round. By the time they were done, an hour had elapsed, and Josie said there would be a twenty-minute break while they conferred and chose the first- and second-place winners in each class.

"We will announce those today," she added. "But the overall prize for Best in Show will be awarded tomorrow, so make sure you're here for both days of the contest!"

Again, people murmured amongst themselves, although in this case, it seemed as if they were more interested in using the small break to hit the food vendors...and to make a run for the beer garden, which appeared to have opened up sometime during the judging.

Obviously, the beer didn't hold much allure for me. But Calvin went and got me a soft pretzel from one of the food stands, along with a bottle of water, while Hazel headed over to another vendor to fetch herself a bag of kettle corn.

"I don't dare take any home, or I'd be eating it all day," she confessed in between bites. "But it's nice to be able to indulge myself while I'm here."

I glanced around and noticed an obvious lack of beer-makers. Somehow, I'd thought they'd be here during the judging. "Where are the competitors?" I asked, then handed my bottle of water over to Calvin so he could have some as well.

"Oh, Josie decided she didn't want them in the audience during the judging because it would be too distracting," Hazel replied. "But they'll be here when today's results are announced. That's why she has that group of seats blocked off over there."

Sure enough, there was a group of five chairs sitting empty at one end of the front row.

"And after the judging," Hazel went on, "they'll all go to their various booths so they can talk one-on-one with people about their beers and their brewing processes. They were actually doing that for a while before the judging started, but Josie shooed them off to the kitchen to be sequestered right before you got here."

Well, Calvin and I had been running a little late. At least this explained why I hadn't seen any of the brewers so far. Unfortunately, this new clarification meant I wouldn't be able to head for home right after the judging but would have to do my best to chat up each of the competitors, or at least do a little surreptitious surveillance, just to see if they acted any differently in public than they had when talking to me in private.

Right after our exchange, the three judges returned to their table, with Henry sending a nod in Josie's direction as if to let her know they were ready to render their verdict for this first round of competition. In turn, she inclined her head to one of the women who'd brought out the beers to be judged, and she hurried off toward the kitchen, apparently so she could fetch the brew-makers and guide them to their seats.

Sure enough, they all made their way to the front row a moment later, while I watched them through narrowed eyes, trying to figure out if I could detect any changes in their demeanor from the last time I'd talked to them. Both Dave Perry and Nick Russell were all smiles, clearly in their element as people clapped and several individuals shouted their names, as if they were rock stars rather than a couple of guys who'd decided to start making beer.

Then again, I knew next to nothing about the world of craft brewing. For all I knew, the two of them were celebrities in their own little circle.

Elijah Wright didn't look nearly as at ease, shoulders slightly slumped as he made his way to his seat. At least he lifted a hand to wave, although he appeared reluctant to do so and had only made the gesture because someone had advised him to be more personable.

Sofia Barnes also appeared almost embarrassed, but she flashed a shy smile at the crowd before hurrying to her seat, and Matt Mitchell only gave a slight nod before he sat down as well. Now all I could see was the backs of their heads, which I knew wasn't going to tell me much.

And I really couldn't read much from their behavior as they'd exited the kitchen, because all of them had reacted to the crowd pretty much exactly the way I'd expected them to.

I tried not to sigh as Henry stood up, a piece of paper in his hands. Josie bustled over to take it from him and he sat down, clearly relieved he wasn't the one who had to make the announcements. Maybe he had to speak in public as a police chief, to give press conferences and whatnot— although our small town generally didn't have anything important enough going on that it would require a press conference—but it still seemed to me he was more than happy to let Josie take over from here.

Her light blue eyes scanned the paper Henry had given her, and she gave a small nod.

"I'm very happy to announce the winners of today's competition," she said, her lapel mic picking up her words and broadcasting them to the waiting audience. "For the lagers, second place goes to Nick Russell for his Desert Mirage lager."

Even from where I sat, I could see Nick Russell's ears turn bright red. He hadn't come across to me as the sort of person who was easily embarrassed, but maybe he wasn't used to receiving public accolades like this.

Looking genuinely shocked, he stood up and let Josie pick up a small trophy from the judges' table and hand it over. "Congratulations," she said, and he nodded, then escaped back to his chair.

"First place in the lager class, Sofia Barnes."

Even though I barely knew her, I had to be

proud that the only woman in the competition had just won a first-place prize. She got up and also claimed a slightly larger trophy than the one Nick had received, and, like her fellow prize winner, quickly returned to her seat. I'd only been able to see her in profile, but it looked as if her cheeks had flushed bright red.

A reaction I got to see two more times, since both her pilsner and her wheat beer also won prizes, second for the pilsner and first for the wheat. Matt Mitchell won first prize for his pilsner, although I noted that none of Elijah's beers had placed in this round. Well, maybe he specialized more in the darker beers and would shine in the competition tomorrow.

After the prizes were awarded, Josie thanked everyone for attending and urged people to eat and visit the beer garden. It didn't look to me as if they needed much encouragement, because a large contingent of the spectators had already surged that way before she was even done speaking.

The brewers also got up from their seats, presumably so they could go to their booths and mingle with the attendees. I wondered if having to be sociable would be tough for people like Elijah and David Perry, who hadn't won anything yet, then decided that David Perry's ego wouldn't allow him to be too disappointed, and Elijah most likely didn't care too much what anyone else thought of him.

As Sofia Barnes stood up, I noticed a tall man with thinning fair hair approach her and murmur something in a low tone. She nodded, a small smile touching her mouth, although she didn't look hugely happy despite making such a good showing in the competition today.

After that brief exchange, the two of them left the judging area, presumably going toward her booth. As they went, I found myself frowning.

Was the fair-haired man Kurt Vonn, her business partner?

Since she obviously hadn't been interested in making introductions, I had no idea.

Well, one way to find out.

I got up from my seat and looked down at my husband. "I think I need to talk to Sofia Barnes again."

THIRTEEN

Jailhouse Rock

HAZEL BEGGED OFF FROM THE conversation— Chuck had just emerged from the judging room, and the two of them wanted to go to the beer garden rather than talk with any brewers—so Calvin and I made our own way toward Sofia's booth. Predictably, it was mobbed, with people wanting to offer her their congratulations or hear in person how she'd been able to dominate the first part of the competition.

However, I wasn't about to let the crowds dissuade me. Eventually, the throng ebbed enough that the two of us were able to approach Sofia just as the fair-haired man I'd spotted earlier was speaking to her, his head bent close.

"Hi, Sofia," I said as Calvin and I approached.

She gave me a surprised smile—most likely, she hadn't been expecting me to attend the judging.

Then she seemed to recover herself and said, "Hi, Selena. This is Kurt, my business partner. Kurt, this is Selena Marx and...."

Her words trailed off as her cheeks flushed light pink—I could tell she remembered meeting Calvin at the reception but couldn't recall his name. Coming to her rescue, I said, "This is my husband, Calvin Standingbear."

The two men shook hands and exchanged greetings. Then Kurt said, "Hate to rush off, but I wanted to grab something to eat for Sofia, since she probably won't have the chance to get away on her own."

He hurried away toward the food stands, and I couldn't help smiling a little. It was the sort of considerate gesture Calvin would have made for me, and I wondered if their relationship was a little bit more intimate than merely being business partners.

Since it would have been extremely rude to ask Sofia that kind of question point-blank, I left my musings on the subject aside for now. "Congratulations on your wins today," I said. "That was pretty impressive."

Again, pink suffused her cheeks. "I was really surprised," she replied, and, judging by her still almost bewildered air, I could see she was telling the simple truth. "I honestly didn't think I was going to place at all. There are some really good brewers here."

"Well, the judges seemed impressed," Calvin put in. "And I personally know that Henry Lewis isn't easy to impress."

Because I knew all about my husband's history with Henry—the two men were cautiously polite to one another on a good day, and that was about it —I had to smother a smile. "No, he isn't," I replied gravely. "And actually, neither is Chuck. He's definitely not one of those guys who'll drink whatever you put in front of him."

I knew a lot less about Brett's drinking habits, mostly because we'd never really socialized. He and his wife were just enough older than Calvin and me, their family already established and their kids in school, that we didn't have much overlap when it came to schedules and interests.

Sofia didn't seem terribly reassured by the bona fides I'd just offered. She reached up to push a wisp of pale blonde hair away from her face, saying, "Well, I'm pretty sure I won't do nearly as well tomorrow. Elijah's really good with the darker brews, while I only really started making them about a year ago."

"You might be surprised," I said, although, since I hadn't drunk any of their offerings, I didn't know whether she was being self-deprecating or whether Elijah really did present her with some serious competition.

Unfortunately, I didn't get the opportunity to say anything more than that, because several couples crowded into the tent, obviously wanting to talk to the woman of the hour, and I knew it would be rude—and way too conspicuous—to deny them their chance for conversation by continuing to monopolize Sofia.

No, I just offered her a smile and headed out, with Calvin right behind me. As we began to walk toward Nick Russell's booth...mostly because it was the one next to Sofia's...we passed Kurt Vonn, who was carrying a sandwich in one of those little cardboard serving trays, with what looked like a soda of some kind in his other hand. He gave us a slight nod, but since he was obviously on a mission to deliver the food to his partner, we didn't try to stop him.

Nick's booth was jammed, though, with him chatting up a couple of attractive women I didn't recognize and who I guessed had driven in from the Phoenix area to attend the competition. Same story at David Perry's display, and I stopped there, frowning a little.

"I don't know if it's worth staying," I said, and Calvin tilted his head.

"You're sure?"

I nodded. "All the brewers are mobbed, and it's

obvious they're talking with the public and not with each other. So, even if I might have been able to pick up on something by watching them interacting, I don't think that's going to happen."

For a moment, my husband was silent, his keen dark eyes scanning the booths. Then he said, "You're right. But I hope you won't think this was a waste of time."

"Well," I said with a limp smile, "I got to see Hazel, and it's good to know that Josie's event went off without a hitch after all. And I'll admit I enjoyed watching Sofia win all those awards, especially when I know that female brewers can have a hard time of it."

"That was good," Calvin agreed. "But I'm fine with going home if you're ready."

I definitely was more than ready to get back to the house and put my feet up, so we joined hands and walked toward the exit, then out to his SUV. By that point, it was almost full dark outside, the days shorter and shorter with the solstice only a week away.

But the inside of the Durango was comfortable enough, thanks to the seat warmers and the hot air that began to blow almost instantly out of the vents, and I knew we had food in the crock pot waiting for us at home. Calvin would light a fire in the hearth, and we could be all snuggly and cozy together.

As wonderful as that image felt to me, though, it didn't get me any closer to learning who really had sneaked up on Trent the other night, beaten him, and then drowned him in that vat. My gut still didn't want to accept that the fentanyl dealer from Goodyear was the culprit, even though Josie and the authorities all seemed to believe they had their man.

As we were turning onto the gravel lane that led to our house, I said, "Do you think they'd let me visit the suspect?"

Calvin sent a surprised glance in my direction before returning his attention to the road. "You mean the drug dealer?"

I nodded.

Silence for a beat or two, and then he said, "Maybe. I mean, he's being held without bail because of his priors, but that shouldn't prevent him from having visitors." Another pause, and my husband added, "That's if he'll even agree to talk to you."

"Oh, he will," I said grimly. "Once he finds out I might be able to help him beat this murder rap."

Calvin must have pulled some strings, although he didn't provide too many details as to how he managed to get me an interview with Manuel

Lorca the next day. All I knew was that, when we arrived at the jail in Goodyear, the deputy on duty was expecting me and ushered me back to the visiting area right away while Calvin waited in the lobby.

"Better for you to talk to him alone," my husband told me, then gave me a kiss on the cheek. "Guys like that can smell a cop from a mile away."

While I might have preferred to have my husband's reassuring presence there during the interview, I could see why he'd made that decision. I nodded, told myself I'd be perfectly fine, and did my best to look cool and composed as I sat down in the chair opposite the little glass partition. The setup looked like something more out of a prison than a regular jail, but then, I had to admit our little Globe police station couldn't really compare to a facility in the big city.

A moment later, Manuel Lorca, wearing an orange jumpsuit, was led to the chair on the opposite side of the glass. I had no idea what I'd been expecting—probably the stereotypical tattooed, shaved-headed gangbanger seen on countless TV shows—but Mr. Lorca definitely wasn't that. Maybe a few years younger than I, he was strikingly handsome, with wavy black hair, regular features, and dark eyes framed by sooty lashes, and looked like he should have been acting in a *telenovela* rather than cooking fentanyl in a half-built brewpub.

After he sat down and we were left alone...well, mostly alone, since the deputy who'd guided me here kept watch at the door and Manuel's own guard stepped back but didn't entirely disappear... he sent me a suspicious look from under those amazing lashes. "Who the hell are you?"

Not the politest of openings, but then, he was under a lot of stress at the moment. "My name is Selena Marx. I wanted to talk to you about Trent Reynolds."

At once, Manuel Lorca's expression seemed to close down. "I didn't kill him."

"I know you didn't," I said calmly, and his dark eyes flared with shock.

"How do you know that?"

"I just do," I responded, still in that neutral tone. "Let's just say I don't believe the evidence stacks up. Do you have an alibi for the time you were supposed to be in Globe, murdering Trent Reynolds?"

"I was hanging with some friends," Manuel replied. "And I told the cops that. But they're not going to take the word of a bunch of people with rap sheets."

Probably not. If Manuel had really wanted a good alibi, he should have been in a Bible study class or something...not that many of those were conducted at three in the morning.

"But did the police talk to them anyway?"

He shrugged. Even in an orange jumpsuit, his broad shoulders were kind of spectacular. I had to wonder why someone who looked like an actor or male model had gotten involved in a life of crime when other avenues must have been open to him.

Or possibly not. Extreme good looks weren't always enough to overcome social and economic pressure.

"The cops talked to a couple of my guys, but they didn't believe anything they said. And because we were just hanging and watching TV and drinking, it's not like we've got receipts to prove we were where we said we were." Manuel paused there, his straight, dark brows pulling together. "Yeah, they think just because he owed me money, that was reason enough to kill him, which is stupid. Homeboy was a lot more valuable to me alive than he was dead. The setup in that kitchen was pretty sweet."

I could imagine. If Scott Doyle's account of his business partner was correct, then Trent liked the finer things in life, and that probably meant getting top-of-the-line equipment for the kitchens in his brewpubs, even if he really couldn't afford it.

Manuel stopped there and gave me another of

those narrow glances. "So...why do you think I didn't do it?"

"Just a feeling," I said. "But I needed to talk to you in person, because right now, the police believe they have the right guy, and that means the real killer is out there walking around somewhere and thinking he's going to get off scot-free. Maybe this was all personal, and now that Trent's dead, the murderer isn't going to strike again. I don't know that for sure, though, which is why it's super-important to figure out who it actually is."

There wasn't even a flicker of expression in Manuel's face as he listened to all this, which didn't surprise me too much. Anyone in his line of work had to be very good at keeping his cards close to his vest.

Not feeling terribly encouraged, I went on, "And that's another reason why I thought I should talk to you, since you and Trent worked together."

Manuel's shoulders lifted again. "I wouldn't call it working. He let me use his space, that's all."

"But you must have had some interactions," I persisted, doing my best to ignore the nagging sensation that maybe Calvin and I had driven all the way out here for nothing.

"A few," Manuel admitted. "Guy was a jerk, you know? Thought he was important because he had the money to open some restaurants. Problem was, he bit off way more than he could chew, which was why he ended up needing my help."

"Were there a lot of people who might have wanted him dead?"

Not even a blink. "Wouldn't surprise me. He was good at pissing people off. One guy showed up at the brewpub about a month ago, saying he wanted to blow Trent's head off for messing with his girl."

Well, that was news. Although, come to think of it, if a guy didn't seem to have a problem stealing other people's beer recipes, he probably also didn't have an issue with trying to take someone's girlfriend as well.

"Were you there when that happened?" I asked.

"No," Manuel replied immediately. "One of my crew told me about it. They got rid of the dude, made it pretty clear it wasn't smart for him to come around there."

I had to wonder if the unknown man had realized he'd stumbled into an illegal fentanyl operation, or whether he'd thought Manuel's crew was just there working on the kitchen. Probably the latter, or I doubted they would have let him walk out of there alive.

"Did they give you a description?"

"They just said it was a white guy."

Well, that narrowed things down. Still, at least it was now established that Trent also had people angry with him for cheating with their girlfriends, which meant I had a whole other set of reasons why someone might have wanted him dead.

And here I'd hoped this interview might help me narrow things down a bit.

"So yeah, I'm not upset that the guy's dead," Manuel went on, in the sort of off-hand tone that told me this wasn't the first time he'd had to deal with a dead partner. "I'm just pissed that the cops think I did it. The drug charges are one thing—I wasn't actually at the brewpub when the cops found the lab, so my lawyer thinks he can make that go away—but I don't want to take the fall for someone else when I wasn't the one who killed him."

Some people might have argued Mr. Lorca was guilty of enough other crimes that it really didn't matter which one sent him to prison for a long time. However, while I definitely wouldn't excuse his actions, I also didn't like the idea of him going to jail for something he didn't do...especially if it meant the real killer would get to walk away from the whole mess and act like it had never happened.

"I'm going to do what I can to get this figured out," I said. "But it would really help me if you could tell me everything you know about Trent Reynolds."

"I already told you," Manuel replied, his tone level. I could tell he knew I wasn't a cop, but he hadn't bothered to ask exactly what I was doing here, either. Maybe in his mind, it didn't matter. "We had an arrangement, that's all. That arrangement worked better for me when he was still alive. So yeah, I didn't have any reason to kill him."

That seemed to be that. I got up from my chair, saying, "Well, thank you for your time, Mr. Lorca."

He smiled, clearly amused. "Right now, I ain't got anything but time."

***

"Still convinced of his innocence?" Calvin asked as we drove away.

"As much as I can be," I replied. It would have been helpful if I could have seen Manuel Lorca's aura...or maybe not. After all, someone with that much mayhem in their life probably had a murky aura even if they weren't a killer. "Sounds to me that, even though Trent owed him money, Manuel didn't have much of a reason to kill him. He did tell me Trent was kind of a player, so now we have to worry about jealous boyfriends and husbands in addition to all the people he stole from."

My husband's mouth quirked. "Sounds like he was a busy guy. I wonder when he even had the time to brew beer."

I had to wonder, too. For all I knew, Trent

Reynolds hired someone to do his brewing for him, in which case, we might have yet another suspect.

Something about the theory didn't ring true, though. He wanted the recognition, wanted to be seen as a big name in the brewing community, and that meant he had to be front and center, making his beer. Maybe he was doing so with stolen formulas, but he was hands-on about the craft portion of the job.

"Well, luckily, Lorca's murder trial hasn't even been scheduled yet, so you have time to figure it out," Calvin remarked.

For some reason, those words didn't reassure me very much. I hated the idea of the real killer out in the world somewhere, free to commit whatever heinous acts he wanted because he knew he would never be suspected of being involved in those crimes.

"I don't like to think an innocent person is being locked up," I said, and my husband chuckled.

"I wouldn't exactly call Manuel Lorca 'innocent.'"

All right, fair enough. "Guilty of this particular crime, then," I said primly, and Calvin's mouth quirked.

"Okay, you got me there," he replied. "But what now? Home?"

As much as I wanted to go back to the house to try to regroup, I knew the answers I was seeking didn't lie there. Sure, I could try breaking out my Tarot cards again, but what would be the point?

They'd already told me what I needed to know.

"No," I said firmly. "Let's go back to the competition."

FOURTEEN

Winners and Losers

WHEN WE GOT BACK TO GLOBE, IT WAS five-thirty, well after the time when the second round of the competition would have started. That was why we had to stand awkwardly toward the back of the judging area, since all the seats had been filled.

Well, it wasn't as if we hadn't been sitting in the car for the past two hours during the drive back from Goodyear.

It looked like Chuck and Henry and Brett had already gone through the first batch of brews, if the single empty half-pint glass in front of each of them was any indication. Luckily, I already knew that today they would be judging pale ale, brown ale, and stout, so I assumed it was the pale ale that had been the first one to be drunk.

They were all scribbling notes as Calvin and I

took our places at the back of the crowd. Since that wasn't the most interesting thing to watch, I craned my head to see if I could make out Hazel in the audience. Yes, there she was, sitting in the front row next to Josie—and Joyce Lewis and Terry Woodrow, who'd probably all gotten places of honor because their husbands were the judges.

No sign of the brewers, though, which meant they'd probably been hustled off to the kitchen while the actual judging was taking place. And since it didn't seem as if any of my friends had yet realized that Calvin and I were here, this felt like the perfect opportunity to do a little sleuthing.

"I'm going to the kitchen," I whispered to Calvin, and he raised an eyebrow.

"Why?"

"Because that's where all the brewers are," I responded in the same undertone, then stepped away before he could offer any objections.

Not that he probably would have. He knew I'd been hoping for a little more face time with the competitors.

Sure enough, when I pushed open the door to the kitchen—after making sure no one seemed to be paying any attention to me—I saw them hanging around in there, Nick leaning against the counter and studying his phone's screen, Matt Mitchell off in a corner talking to his wife, David

Perry attempting to chat up Sofia, who looked as though she'd rather be just about anywhere else.

The only person I didn't see was Elijah Wright.

"Hi," I said as I stuck my head in. "I just thought I'd see how all of you are doing. Does anyone need some water or anything else?"

The four of them appeared somewhat startled, as if they couldn't quite figure out why the woman who'd been grilling them about Trent's death only a few days earlier was now apparently acting as Josie's assistant.

In response, David brandished the bottle of water he'd been holding down at one side. "We're covered, thanks. How's the judging going?"

"It looks like they're only about a third of the way through," I replied. "So there's a ways to go."

He didn't appear too thrilled by my answer, although I could tell Sofia was relieved by my presence, since it had distracted David from his all-too-obvious attempts to flirt with her.

Since I could practically cut the awkwardness in the room with a butter knife, I ventured, "Where's Elijah? Weren't you all supposed to stay in here together?"

Nick shoved his phone in his jeans pocket. "He was stressing majorly, so he went outside to have a smoke."

Considering it was in the low fifties outside, with

a chilly wind blowing down from the north, that must have been some nicotine habit. Or, since I really hadn't noticed a scent of smoke on his clothes when I visited him at his Airbnb a few days earlier, maybe it was something he only did in times of extreme pressure.

Smiling, I said, "I'll just go check on him, then," and made my way past the group and through the door that opened on the rear parking lot. Sure enough, Elijah was standing on the walkway, moodily smoking a cigarette as he stared across the lot and into the open field on the other side. People had been debating for years what should be done with that unused lot, but since no one seemed to agree on a solution, it had continued to remain empty.

As soon as Elijah caught sight of me, though, he dropped the cigarette on the ground and put it out with his foot. "Sorry," he said. "It's kind of a disgusting habit."

"It's fine," I assured him. Although I couldn't stand the scent of cigarette smoke and definitely didn't want to be inhaling it in my current condition, I kind of doubted it would have done me much harm out there in the open air, especially with that brisk wind blowing, one that made me glad I still wore my mohair wrap over my sweater dress.

"Is Josie having you ride herd on us?" he asked

next, an ironic smile lifting one corner of his mouth.

"Something like that," I said, figuring the little lie wouldn't hurt anyone. "They're doing the judging right now, so it should only be another twenty minutes or so."

"Twenty minutes too long," Elijah replied. "I didn't want to deal with being cooped up in there with everyone, so I figured I'd wait it out here where I could get some fresh air."

Some people might have debated the usefulness of "fresh air" when it was being breathed in at the same time as cigarette smoke, but I knew I wouldn't comment.

"Waiting can be uncomfortable," I agreed.

"And it didn't help that David kept trying to hit on Sofia," Elijah went on. "That guy is seriously clueless."

This was exactly the kind of information I'd been hoping to pick up, telling me I'd done the right thing by coming out here to talk to Elijah Wright. Maybe our conversation still wouldn't guide me to the killer, but at least I might be able to get some insights into how this little group inter-acted with each other.

"Why's that?" I asked.

Elijah looked as though he regretted stubbing out his cigarette. "Because she's with Kurt, her partner. Sounds like it's been going on almost as long as they've been working together."

Ah...that explained a lot. Why they'd been talking in hushed tones with each other, why he'd gone to fetch her some food to keep her energy levels up. Yes, it seemed like he was probably at least seven or eight years older than she was, but in the grand scheme of things, I supposed it wasn't such a huge age difference.

"And David doesn't know about it?"

Elijah made a disgusted noise. "Of course he does. But since he thinks he's God's gift to women, he probably thought he could get her to leave Kurt and come work with him. You know, join forces and brew together. Never mind she would never do that...or that David would be the one reaping the most benefit from the situation, since she's a much better brewer than he is."

Interesting. Since my companion seemed willing to talk, I was going to do my best to keep things going. It was entirely possible his chattiness had everything to do with trying to keep his mind off the judging currently taking place in the building behind us, but still, I wouldn't look a gift horse in the mouth.

"David does seem pretty popular," I ventured, and Elijah shook his head.

"With people who don't know better," he said. "Sofia can see right through him. I'm not surprised she did as well as she did yesterday, but those are the beers she does best. I know I can take her in the judging today."

Since I'd never tasted any of either Elijah's or Sofia's beers, I wouldn't try to guess which way the judges might lean. I made a sound I hoped was noncommittal without being dismissive, and apparently it worked, because Elijah spoke again.

"With that ten grand, I can buy a better bottling machine, be able to get my stuff in more venues. There's a lot of competition for shelf space, but a win here would help me get the word out that much more."

"Even in New Mexico?" I asked, wondering if winning a small brewing contest in Globe, Arizona, would really "get the word out."

"Even in New Mexico," Elijah responded with one of his rare smiles. "People pay attention. Whereas Sofia really doesn't need the money, not with Kurt Vonn bankrolling her."

It would have been crass to ask whether Sofia's business partner and significant other was rolling in dough. Instead, I said, "Well, it does help to have someone with funds backing you, I suppose."

A brief nod. "I guess it worked out for Sofia, except...."

"Except what?"

His shoulders lifted. "I don't talk about other

people's business. It just seems to me she could have done better."

Before I could find the words to respond—was Elijah dismissive of Kurt Vonn because he was jealous, or had he made the comment because he'd noticed something off about their relationship?—the door to the kitchen opened, and Matt Mitchell stuck his head out.

"The judging's over. Josie wants us to go take our seats."

At once, Elijah's posture became even more tense, and yet again, I was struck by how much this competition meant to him. "Guess we'd better go in," he said, the casual note in his voice not fooling me for one second.

I nodded, and we both went inside. The warmth of the kitchen contrasted sharply with the icy wind out in the parking lot, and I found myself glad we'd been called in, although Elijah hadn't seemed to notice the chill.

The other brewers had already gone into the gymnasium, so the two of us headed in there as well, although Elijah made a beeline for his empty seat in the front row, while I hung back and joined Calvin where he was still standing behind the spectators.

"Learn anything?" he asked, pitching his voice low so the people seated in front of us wouldn't be able to hear what we were saying.

I gave a helpless little shrug. "I'm not sure. I get the feeling that Elijah doesn't have much use for Sofia's business partner."

"Jealous?" Calvin asked, echoing my own thoughts of just a few minutes earlier.

And the image of the King of Pentacles reversed flashed into my mind. The card reading had indicated jealousy of some kind, but even if Elijah had a thing for Sofia...which I wasn't sure he did...why would he have killed Trent rather than Kurt, if he wanted to make a play for her himself?

None of this was making any sense.

"I don't know," I said. "This whole thing feels murkier than swamp water. There are...undercurrents...for lack of a better word, but I don't know what they're supposed to mean."

Calvin took my hand where it was hanging down at my side and gave it a gentle squeeze, clearly his way of letting me know that he still believed in me, even if I was feeling utterly stymied at the moment. We didn't have time for any further conversation, though, because Josie, resplendent in an emerald green dress with a holiday scarf depicting red and green and gold bells swathed around her neck, had made her way to her usual spot in front of the judges' table.

The rest of the crowd quieted down as well, and she smiled at everyone. I noticed that she held a piece of paper in one hand, which I guessed contained the results of today's judging...and the name of the person who'd won the overall grand prize and its accompanying ten thousand dollars.

"Thank you to everyone for being with us on the second day of the inaugural High Country Holiday Brewing Competition," she said. "The judges have made their decisions, but I just wanted to say that all of the brewers competing this weekend are working at the very top of their game, and I wish we could have awards for each and every one of them. Let's give them a big round of applause!"

The crowd began to clap, and Calvin let go of my hand so we could join in as well. As I glanced around, all I could see was people who looked happy to be here...and why shouldn't they be? As far as they knew, Trent Reynolds' killer was safely locked up in jail, and that meant the rest of us could relax and join in celebrating the brewers who were competing today.

I only wished I could be so nonchalant about the whole situation.

But I managed to stand there and look happy and interested in the results of the judging. Actually, I *was* interested, mostly because I wanted to know whether Sofia Barnes would make as good a showing today, and whether she'd be able to eclipse the rest of her competitors and take home that grand prize.

"In the brown ale category," Josie said, then paused for dramatic effect. "Second place—Sofia Barnes!"

Everyone clapped, and she rose from her seat to take her award. I scanned the crowd but couldn't see any sign of Kurt Vonn. Was he glad she'd been able to place in a category that wasn't one of her top strengths, or annoyed she hadn't done better?

Josie glanced down at the paper she held, although I guessed she already knew by heart who had won every category. "And first place for his Pueblo Pale Ale," she intoned, "Elijah Wright!"

I hadn't exactly been holding my breath, but something inside me relaxed at hearing those words. While I still didn't know quite what to make of Mr. Wright, I realized I'd still been secretly rooting for him to win, considering he hadn't placed yesterday at all.

Elijah also won first place in the brown ale and stout categories, while David Perry came in second with his Four Peaks brown ale, and Matt Mitchell took second for his Midnight Mesa stout. That meant everyone had won at least one prize. Had it really shaken out that way, or were the judges just trying to spread the love around?

I told myself that Chuck and Henry and Brett were all people who believed in playing fair, so I didn't think they would have done anything under-handed while deciding who should win which prize. No, this was just how things had turned out, and I was glad for all the competitors, glad that no one would be going home with nothing to show for their efforts.

"And now," Josie went on, after everyone had returned to their seats, trophies in hand, "this is the moment we've all been waiting for—grand prize in the competition, and an award of ten thousand dollars. I'm sure all our competitors have a long list of things they'd like to use that money for."

An amused little murmur ran through the crowd, although I noticed the brewers sat still and silent in their seats, waiting for Josie's announcement. This wasn't the sort of thing they could joke about, not when getting an amount like that with no strings attached could allow them to do so much to improve their businesses.

"This was very difficult," she said, and I got the feeling she was trying to string things out to keep the suspense building. "Our judges deliberated for quite some time before they finally settled on our overall winner. And that person is"—a long pause for dramatic effect—"Elijah Wright!"

I blinked. Right then, I wasn't sure whether to be happy for Elijah or sad for Sofia, and decided I could be a little of both.

Elijah, on the other hand, was wearing the sort of wide grin that I doubted graced his saturnine face very often, and he shook Josie's hand with the kind of energy he probably only employed when he was stirring his latest mash. She smiled back at him, then nodded at Henry, who got up from his seat and handed over an envelope, one I assumed must hold the cashier's check for the prize money.

"Did you see that coming?" Calvin murmured to me, and I shook my head.

"Not really. I mean, I got the feeling that Elijah and Sofia were the two most skilled brewers here, but personal taste is so subjective. I'm happy for him, though. I know winning here meant a lot to him."

Things got kind of confused at the front of the judging area—Henry and Chuck and Brett were now all standing and talking to the various competitors, and the crowd surged toward them as well, as if everyone in attendance wanted to offer their own congratulations. However, some of Calvin's off-duty deputies were able to prevent the brewers from getting completely swarmed, and to direct people away from the competitors and over to the booths and the food stands and the beer garden.

Because of the ebb and flow of the crowd, I was able to catch a glimpse of Kurt Vonn, who didn't look very happy. I couldn't really blame him— while the money might not have meant as much to their operation, I had to believe Sofia winning the grand prize here probably would have lent their brewing business some much-needed cachet.

He moved forward to the spot where Sofia was standing with her fellow competitors. Obviously, I couldn't hear what he said, but it looked as though he bent down and murmured something in her ear. Possibly, it was some kind of reassurance, because she managed a smile as she looked up at him.

That was all I was able to see, since several more people crowded close despite the security team trying to keep the crowds at bay. I hesitated for a moment, wondering if it would be the polite thing to stay and congratulate Elijah, and to find Josie and let her know she'd done a wonderful job of pulling off the whole thing despite the odds.

At the moment, though, I couldn't help but feel an overwhelming sense of defeat. The competition was over, even if the social part of the evening would continue for a few more hours, and I still hadn't been able to figure out who really had killed Trent Reynolds in this very spot only a few nights ago.

My fingers found Calvin's again. "Let's go home," I said.

FIFTEEN

Calculated Risks

"YOU'RE VERY QUIET," CALVIN REMARKED once we were out of the old high school's parking lot and headed toward home.

"Sorry," I said. "I just...this is the first time I've failed." He raised an eyebrow, and I went on, "I promised Josie I would find the killer before the competition started, and I didn't do that. Hell, I couldn't even find him before it ended!"

Because he was in the middle of making a left turn, Calvin couldn't reach out and give my hand a reassuring squeeze the way he normally would have. "I think you're being kind of hard on yourself, Selena," he replied. "You gave yourself an impossible deadline on this one. All those other cases, you had at least a week to solve them, often more. Trying to get this whole thing figured out in just thirty hours? We all knew that was a long shot."

While his words seemed sensible enough, I wasn't sure whether I was willing to accept them. Not when I knew in my gut that Manuel Lorca hadn't killed Trent, and that meant the real perpetrator was still out there somewhere.

Then again, my gut hadn't always been the most reliable thing in the world...not lately, anyway. I'd thought I was feeling better and that the brain fog which seemed to have clouded my judgment only a few weeks earlier had disappeared, but what if I'd only been fooling myself this whole time? What if I still didn't know what the hell I was doing?

"Maybe," I allowed, since I knew sitting there in stony silence wasn't a very good way to respond to my husband, who'd only been trying to help.

Correctly interpreting my mood, he said, "How about we go home, put on a fire and make some spiced cider, have some of those cranberry walnut bars you made the other day? It'll ruin our dinner, but who cares?"

I reached over and laid a hand on his leg, feeling it firm and well-muscled and utterly reassuring beneath my fingertips. "That sounds like a great idea. And if we get hungry for real food, we can make some omelets or something."

"It's a plan."

With that settled, I rested against the seat back and pulled in a breath, trying to tell myself that not solving this particular crime wasn't the end of the world. Or at least, I could give myself the grace to relax just this one night, and try to figure it all out in the morning.

I had to hope that would be enough.

We did have a restful, low-key evening, but in the background, my brain kept pushing at the problem, trying to see if there was some clue I'd overlooked, something that would have sent me in the right direction but which I'd missed, for whatever reason.

However, no matter how much I picked at the problem, I couldn't seem to come up with any one detail that stood out in particular. Now I understood why all those crazy conspiracy theory types had those big bulletin boards with their numerous clues and connecting pieces of red string—otherwise, it would be nearly impossible to keep up with it all.

I thought I did a pretty good job of convincing Calvin I was willing to let it go for now, and we ate cranberry squares—and later, grilled cheese, since we decided that was easier than making omelets—before watching some silly holiday rom-com and calling it a night. He went to sleep almost immediately, while I lay there and stared up into the dark, listening to his deep, even breaths and feeling Sadie's warm little body pressed against my leg.

My thoughts drifted back to the cards: the King of Pentacles, the reversed Queen of Pentacles, and the Chariot...also reversed. Jealousy, a possible lawsuit.

Well, there had been a real lawsuit, the one Elijah had brought against Trent for stealing his Chile Whisperer IPA formula. But still, even though I doubted anyone would have nominated Trent Reynolds for citizen of the year, it didn't feel as if jealousy had motivated his theft of the recipe. No, he'd just wanted to make sure he was making the kind of beer that would bring people to his brewpubs and didn't quite trust that he had the chops to accomplish such a thing on his own.

And Elijah had come out on top, winning the grand prize in the brewing competition. I had to believe his fellow competitors were probably plenty jealous tonight, but those awards had been handed out long after I performed that card reading. Then again, the Tarot looked everywhere, to the past, present, and future. It could be it had been trying to tell me about the jealousy that would arise after the contest winner was announced, but that interpretation didn't feel right to me, not when I'd specifically asked about Trent's murder and not the competition.

I thought then of all the brewers, how none of them had really seemed like murder suspects to me. True, a large part of that assessment was based on my analysis of their auras and nothing else, but my auras, although they couldn't be called on command, were pretty much always accurate.

Because I didn't want to disturb Calvin as he slept, I couldn't let out the annoyed breath that rose to my lips. No, I had to lie there and pick at the problem, and try to figure out where I'd gone wrong.

Unfortunately, there were probably hundreds of details I'd overlooked, connections I hadn't made. With so many possible suspects, it was very hard to narrow things down so my suspicions could land on one person and one person alone.

Let it alone, I told myself. *Stressing like this isn't good for you or the baby.*

Well, that was true enough. I placed one hand against my belly, felt the curve of flesh that had been flat only six months ago, sensing the energy and the will of the being I carried within me. Somehow, feeling it there made me relax a little, as if my child had whispered to me, *It's going to be okay.*

I decided I would let myself believe that.

It was still dark when my eyelids fluttered open. I shifted in bed and glanced over at the clock.

Five thirty-seven.

Much earlier than I would have preferred to be awake, even though I knew it could have been worse. Today, Calvin had to be at the station at eight o'clock, meaning he'd be waking up soon anyway.

However, I wanted him to sleep a little longer.

I slid out from under the covers, grabbed my robe from where it hung just inside the door to the walk-in closet, and then went down the short hallway to my office. To my relief, Sadie hadn't stirred, but she often waited to get up until both of us were out of bed, especially on a cold winter morning like this one.

After I closed my office door, I turned on the overhead light and made my way to the bookcase so I could fetch my Everyday Witch cards. Quite possibly, it was foolish to be going to the Tarot again when all my previous efforts to get it to help me further with Trent Reynolds' murder had been in vain, but I didn't know what else to do.

I shuffled the deck for a long time, waiting to experience the little tingle that usually told me I'd gotten to the place where I needed to stop. For all I knew, it would never appear, and I'd have to accept the sad fact that the cards weren't going to offer any more assistance than they already had.

But then I felt that telltale twinge in my fingertips and I paused, drawing one card from my deck and laying it down on my altar cloth.

The King of Cups.

The card showed a blond man sitting on a throne that looked as if it had been made of tusks or possibly bones, a cup in one hand and a telescope in the other. In this particular case, I wasn't sure what the iconography was supposed to imply, since Globe was hundreds of miles away from any ocean. Generally, the King of Cups was a positive card, albeit one that warned the querent not to separate themselves too much from others. It could also indicate a person of power in your life, but I still couldn't quite figure out its significance in the mystery I was trying to solve.

Well, sometimes I didn't get it right on the first try.

The King of Cups went back into the deck, and I shuffled again...and again...and again...until I experienced that little tingle for a second time. I cut the deck and pulled out the card that felt right in my hand again.

Once more, the King of Cups stared at me, expression almost blank, as if his gaze was fixed on something many miles away.

Clearly, the universe was trying to tell me this was the card I needed to see right now. But why?

Sometimes the card merely stood in for a blond

man, but none of the brewing competition's contestants was fair-haired. Nick Russell and Dave Perry both had sandy hair with lighter streaks, and yet I didn't think anyone would ever consider them truly blond.

No, the only blonde in the competition was Sofia Barnes, but if the cards were trying to point to her, why not show me the Queen of Cups instead of the King?

And then it hit me with almost the impact of a physical blow.

Yes, Sofia Barnes had very light hair...but so did Kurt Vonn.

And Kurt was definitely an authority figure in Sofia's life, whether or not she would admit such a thing openly.

He was also tall enough and strong enough—well, in appearance, anyway—that it wasn't too much of a stretch for me to imagine him beating Trent into unconsciousness and then sticking his head into that vat of water.

Beyond the logistics of such a horrible, cold-blooded murder, however, lay the inevitable question.

Why?

If Kurt had merely been seeking to rid himself of someone he thought was an obstacle to Sofia winning the competition, then one would think Elijah would have been the much more likely target, since most people seemed to be in agreement that he was currently operating at the top of his game. But no one had attacked Elijah, and he'd cruised to victory pretty handily yesterday evening.

Even though I'd been questioning my instincts the day before, they all seemed ready to chime in now and let me know I was on the right track.

What if I'd come to this conclusion too late, though? What if Sofia and Kurt had packed it in last night after the competition and had already driven home to Flagstaff?

I tried to reassure myself that shouldn't be a problem—after all, even if they'd departed from Globe the night before, it wasn't like they'd left the state or something.

Right now, though, I knew I didn't have enough evidence to send the police after Kurt Vonn, which meant I desperately needed to talk to Sofia Barnes in private to see if she could shed some light on why her business partner had felt compelled to murder Trent Reynolds in such a terrible, calculating way.

And that was something I couldn't do if she'd already left town.

A soft knock on the door, and then Calvin stuck his head into my office. "Hey...everything all right?"

"I'm not sure," I said as I shuffled the King of

Cups back into my deck. "But I hope to find out real soon."

Under normal circumstances, I would never have reached out to Josie before ten in the morning. These weren't normal circumstances, however, and although I waited for enough time to elapse while I ate some breakfast and then took a shower, it was still only a little past eight—and right after Calvin's Durango had backed out of the driveway—that I made the call.

I'd told him about my suspicions, of course, because we didn't keep those sorts of secrets from one another. He'd only asked that I not meet with Kurt Vonn unaccompanied, a promise I easily made. There was no way in the world I'd ever allow myself to be alone with someone I thought could be capable of such a horrible crime.

Instead, I'd assured Calvin that I'd try to figure out some way to talk to Sofia with Kurt occupied elsewhere, and that I first needed to determine whether or not the two of them were even still in town.

Hence, the call to Josie.

"Selena!" she exclaimed after she answered her phone. "Is everything all right?"

"I don't know," I replied, which seemed like a

valid enough answer to me. "I mean, I'm fine. But do you know whether Kurt Vonn and Sofia Barnes are still here in Globe?"

A faint, surprised silence, followed by, "I believe so. Both Mavis and Hazel set it up with the brewers so they'd be able to stay in their Airbnbs through noon today, mostly so they wouldn't have to leave right after the contest and be driving late at night." She paused, then asked, "Why do you want to know?"

Although I'd considered telling Josie about my suspicions, I'd ultimately decided it was better to keep them to myself for now. Those card pulls early this morning all seemed to point directly toward Kurt Vonn, but the only way I'd be able to confirm that my guess about his guilt was correct would be to talk to Sofia and see if she could provide any illumination as to why her business partner might have been motivated to get rid of Trent Reynolds in such a terrible and final way.

Unfortunately, I hadn't come up with a really good excuse to hand Josie, which was why I found myself stammering, "Um, well...I just wanted to have a chance to talk to her before she leaves town. She did so well at the competition, and I wanted to see if she was possibly interested in starting a brewpub here in Globe. I thought it was a good idea, even if Trent Reynolds obviously won't be able to do it."

A brief, startled silence followed my comment; although I'd certainly donated to various charities around town and had done what I could to make the money I'd inherited do some good in the world, I'd never once mentioned that I might be interested in assisting budding entrepreneurs.

But then Josie said, "That's a wonderful idea. Globe's a long way from Flagstaff, of course, but I think it would be doable. Let me get you her number."

She paused there, probably so she could pull her phone away from her ear and look up Sofia's number in her contacts list. Then she said, "Here it is—928-555-4127."

Because I was calling Josie from my office, it was easy enough to grab a pen and jot down Sofia's phone number. "Thank you so much, Josie," I said. "Do you have any idea when Sofia and Kurt were going to head back up to Flagstaff?"

Please don't tell me they wanted to get an early start, I thought then, just before Josie responded, "It sounded like they planned to get breakfast here in town before they got on the road. So I don't think they've gone anywhere yet."

That was a piece of good news, although now I'd have to maneuver around them going out to eat. Still, if they planned to be leisurely about their departure, I should have enough time to intercept Sofia somehow.

However, even though I wasn't going to wait until ten to contact her, I knew it was way too early to call or even text. Maybe reaching out around nine would be early enough to get in touch without seeming completely desperate...even though that's exactly what I was.

"Thanks, Josie," I said again. "I'll let you know how our meeting went."

She told me she was looking forward to it and hoped I'd have some good news for her. We ended the call there, and I set down my phone and wondered what I should do with my next half-hour until it was safe to reach out to Sofia Barnes.

I ended up doing some minor chores around the house, took Sadie for a walk, and sat and watched the clock until 9 a.m. came and went. Then I went into my office, picked up my phone, and sent a quick text.

Hi, Sofia. This is Selena Marx—Josie gave me your number. I have a business proposition for you, but I'd really like to talk privately. Could you meet me at my shop on Bridge Street this morning before you leave town? This needs to be just between the two of us.

Then I sent it off, wondering if I sounded like a complete whack job, and whether Sofia would immediately think something was strange because of my insistence on meeting alone. Problem was, I absolutely could not have this conversation with her if Kurt was anywhere around.

A few minutes of tense silence passed, during which I wondered if she was going to blow me off entirely. But then my phone pinged, and I released a relieved breath.

Kurt and I were just about to go for breakfast. But I can meet you after I drop him off at our Airbnb. What's the address to your store?

I sent it to her, explaining that she'd need to come in the back entrance because we wouldn't be technically open for business, thanks to the broken shop window.

Luckily, she didn't ask for any details regarding the window. If she had, I probably would have just told her I was at the store waiting for the glazier to come by and give me an estimate for the repairs. Of course, they weren't slated to come over until the following day, but Sofia didn't need to know that.

It'll probably be around ten-thirty. See you then.

And that seemed to be that.

I sent another text to Hazel, letting her know I planned to keep the shop closed until the window was repaired, since I hadn't made a definite determination about what to do when I'd last spoken with her. That meant losing some valuable shopping days right before Christmas, but I really didn't want customers in the store with that piece of plywood covering the picture window. Not only did it look ugly, but it made the place feel dark and closed in and definitely wasn't conducive to a happy holiday shopping experience.

Even though I knew Sofia wouldn't be arriving until close to ten-thirty, I went ahead and drove into town anyway, figuring I could at least putter around the shop and get a few minor tasks done. Because Hazel had been handling everything herself on Friday and things had been busy, I guessed she hadn't been able to deal with much in the way of inventory or even tidying up.

Which proved to be the case when I got there, so I put the books on the shelves back in order, straightened the little bowls of small tumbled crystals I kept on one display table, and dusted the entire place. It felt good to be so industrious, although bending down to reach the lower shelves on my bookcase was just awkward enough that I knew I wouldn't be able to manage it at all in a month or two.

Then I heard a soft knock at the door that opened into the little foyer just off the parking lot, and turned around to see Sofia there. As soon as our eyes met, she gave a little wave, and I beckoned her to come into the shop.

"I'm so glad you could meet me," I said. "How was breakfast?"

"It was good," she replied. "Kurt and I went to a place called The Flatiron. Their pancakes were terrific."

The Flatiron did make great breakfasts. But with those pleasantries out of the way, I knew I needed to get to the heart of the matter.

"There's no way to say this easily," I went on. "I really needed you to come here so we could talk without Kurt around."

Rather than appear mystified by my comment, Sofia went very still, as if some part of her was reluctantly acknowledging a terrible fact she'd been doing her best to ignore.

Despite the shift in her posture, she said, "Why didn't you want Kurt hearing what you had to say?"

"Because," I said simply, "I'm pretty sure he's the one who killed Trent Reynolds."

SIXTEEN

The Brew That Is True

FOR A SECOND, SOFIA STARED AT ME IN shock. Then she seemed to find her voice and said, "That's crazy. Why would you even think something so horrible?"

Just the sort of protest I'd expected. However, something in her tone didn't feel quite as forceful as it should be, telling me that she'd harbored her own doubts...even if she hadn't wanted to admit them to herself.

"Because it makes sense," I said. "I'm just missing one piece of the puzzle. Why would Kurt be jealous of Trent Reynolds?"

Sofia was very fair, with light skin and blonde hair and clear blue eyes. Now she looked so pale, I worried she might be about to faint.

"Do you need to sit down?" I asked, and at once, she shook her head.

"No—no, I'm okay." She took a deep breath, then said, "It was just a crazy fling. It didn't mean anything."

Now it was my turn for my eyes to widen with shock. "You had an affair with Trent?"

"I—" A pause, and then she sent me a rueful little smile. "I think 'affair' makes it sound way more important than it really was. Trent and I met at a brewing symposium in Tempe last spring. Kurt couldn't come because he was in the middle of meeting with investors up in Flagstaff. So...I went by myself. And Trent...." She stopped there and shook her head. "He was a big flirt. Totally different from Kurt, and I liked the attention. Also, Kurt and I had been fighting a lot, and honestly, I was on the verge of breaking up with him and going it alone, even though trying to stay in the business without his backing would have been tough."

Her voice shook a little, and I could see how hard it was for her to tell me these intimate details. Still, I had to admire her for not holding back, or trying to make her own actions sound better than they had been.

"How did he find out?" I asked, and Sofia lifted her chin.

"I told him," she said. "I hate keeping secrets, and since things were already rocky between us, I thought it would be better to clear the air and let him know what had happened so he could decide what he wanted to do going forward. But he told me he understood, that he'd been an ass lately and he'd try to make it up to me."

This all sounded very noble...except for the part where the person making those noble gestures had ended up drowning his rival in a brewing vat.

"Did he?"

Sofia's mouth twisted. "At first. But then he started using my cheating as something to hold over my head, to make it sound as if I was wrong about everything instead of making one stupid mistake." Her fingers played with the hem of her dark green sweater, a fidgety gesture that I doubted she even realized she was doing. "His behavior was getting pretty old, to be honest, and again I started thinking it was time to end things between us. But then he found out about this contest and thought it would be a great way to get more recognition, and maybe also help our relationship."

She stopped there, frowning, and I wondered if the same idea had just occurred to her as it had to me.

"Do you think....?" she began, then pressed her lips together, as though she didn't want such terrible words to escape them.

Well, I didn't have an emotional connection to Kurt Vonn, so I didn't mind saying it out loud.

"Yes," I said quietly. "I think that must have

been when Kurt got the idea to kill Trent. He encouraged you to compete in the contest so there would be a reason to get near the man you had a fling with."

Now Sofia crossed her arms, almost as if she was hugging herself. Nerves, or maybe simply that it was chillier than usual in the shop, thanks to that piece of plywood allowing plenty of cold December air to slip past it.

"But...." She stopped herself, again giving one of those small shakes of her head. "The timeline doesn't work. Kurt wasn't even here the night Trent was killed. I know he was up at our house in Flagstaff, because we FaceTimed and I could clearly see our living room in the background."

For just a second, I wavered, remembering how Sofia had remarked right when I first met her that her business partner would be coming down the next day with the brew they'd recently bottled.

Except....

"The police think Trent was killed around three in the morning," I said. "What time did you talk to Kurt?"

"About ten, I think," Sofia replied, eyes narrowing slightly as she appeared to pull up her memory of the exchange.

"It's only a little more than three hours from Flagstaff to Globe," I reminded her. "Which would have given him plenty of time to get here and do the deed. Afterward, he'd probably just parked his van somewhere to wait it out so he could bring the beer to your Airbnb in the morning."

"All right, I guess the timeline makes sense," she said, even as she raised her hands in a helpless gesture. "But nothing else does. I mean, who kills a guy over a one-night stand?"

Although I personally didn't know anyone who'd done anything like that—and had never investigated that kind of crime of passion—I had to believe it was a more common occurrence than people might have wanted to believe. Also, the way Kurt had cajoled Sofia to stay with him, then browbeaten her afterward, sounded like classic abuser behavior to me.

And the last thing an abuser wanted was someone horning in on the woman he regarded as his personal property, even if the other man probably hadn't regarded the encounter as anything more than a quick bit of fun. It definitely hadn't been a love for the ages or anything close to it.

The uncharitable thought crossed my mind that the only person Trent Reynolds had ever loved unreservedly was himself.

"Someone who wanted to keep you for his own," I replied, and Sofia made a disgusted sound.

"I don't belong to anybody," she declared, although I thought I detected a hint of false bravado in her voice.

"No," I said, then went on, "but does Kurt know that?"

A long silence, during which she glanced down at the scuffed boots she was wearing. "I don't know," she responded.

It seemed obvious to me she was now confronting issues about her partner that she'd spent way too much time ignoring. "Another question," I said next. "Do you think Kurt is capable of this kind of violence?"

Another of those pauses, this time stretching so long that I was almost sure she was about to tell me none of it was my business, and that she was going to leave.

But then she released a weary little sigh and said in a very small voice, "Maybe. I hate to say that, but...maybe. He never hit me, but there've been a couple of times when he was really angry about something and he'd punch a hole in the wall, or slam the door and take off in his car. I was always the most freaked out then, because I couldn't help worrying that he might get in an accident or have some kind of road rage incident. That might have been part of the reason why I never wanted to have a pet with him—we both just said that we worked such long hours, it wouldn't be fair to have a dog, but in my case, I couldn't help wondering if he might hurt an animal in some way. It just seemed safer not to get one."

Listening to all this, my heart ached for her. I didn't know how she'd ended up with Kurt, what it was in her own heart or her soul that made her believe she should put up with such terrible treatment. I couldn't help thinking of my relationship with Calvin, how he showed how much he loved me in the hundred thoughtful little things he did for me each and every day. Knowing how wonderful love could be, I hated to think not everyone else got to experience that kind of joy, day in and day out.

Sofia stood there, her slender body still, and remained silent for a few moments. I was quiet as well, knowing she needed to work this out on her own and decide what to do next. Her decision had to come from within her and not from anyone else.

Then she looked up, her eyes meeting mine. Sadness there, but also determination...and a growing anger.

"All right," she said. "What do we do next?"

Kurt Vonn vigorously denied everything, of course, but after Henry and his deputies found a hose in the back of his van—a hose that still had water trapped in its coils whose mineral content and salinity matched the water that came out of the faucets in the old high school's kitchen—the pieces began to fall into place. He'd known about Trent's wish to get into the gym and work on his booth after the reception was over, because Sofia had mentioned it to him during their FaceTime conversation earlier that evening.

And because Kurt had already been stewing over how exactly to murder his rival, he immediately realized Trent had given him the perfect setup. An alibi was already in place, thanks to talking to Sofia that very evening, proving he was at home in Flagstaff. Since he knew the setups of the competitors' booths, he also knew there would be a big, empty vat sitting in Trent's display area. Drowning apparently had appealed to Kurt because it was much harder to trace than a bullet or poison.

Currently, he was being held in a jail cell at the police station, and the judge had denied bail due to the viciousness and premeditation of the crime. I tried to get Henry to let me talk to Kurt, but he turned me down flat.

"This isn't like the Melanie Knowles case," he told me, gray eyes looking flintier than ever. "You weren't personally involved."

"But Kurt Vonn smashed my window," I protested. "I'd say that was personal."

Henry wouldn't budge, though. "And the vandalism has been added to the list of charges. We'll let a jury of Mr. Vonn's peers decide what to do about that."

Since I knew I wasn't going to get the police chief to change his mind, I told him I understood, then headed off to my shop, even as I consoled myself that a conversation with Kurt Vonn probably wouldn't have yielded much fruit. If he was continuing to stonewall the police and the assistant D.A., I kind of doubted he would reveal all to me.

After Kurt was arrested late Tuesday morning, word got out quickly, as it always did, with Josie dropping by the shop just as the glaziers were about to get to work repairing the shop window. It turned out they had the glass in stock, so they'd been able to come by the very next day after taking the necessary measurements.

"Did you ever figure out who did that?" she asked, tilting her head toward the place where four burly men were carefully lifting the replacement glass into position.

"Oh, it was Kurt, too," I said, and she blinked in surprise.

"Why in the world would Kurt Vonn want to break your window?"

"To distract me," I replied. "I guess he heard about my hobby of solving crimes, and he thought it would be a good idea to try freaking me out by throwing a rock in here. Unfortunately for him, I don't scare easily."

"That's for sure," Josie agreed. From the look on her face, I got the feeling she was recalling the times when I'd confronted murderers face to face... or participated in entirely unpleasant activities like trying to get an arsenic sample from the local dump.

I hadn't done anything so dangerous this time around, of course, because I had my baby's safety to think of, and not merely mine. Still, it wasn't until Henry also found black leather gloves, a black knitted scarf, and a black backpack in Kurt's truck that I'd put two and two together, since the culprit himself hadn't confessed to the crime and continued to maintain his innocence on that front. However, no one could deny that Mr. Vonn was the same height and build as the man who'd been captured on my security cameras, even if his face had been covered by the scarf.

The evidence was pretty circumstantial, but at least that hadn't prevented Henry from getting the vandalism of my store added to the charges Kurt Vonn was facing. If he was found guilty, then I might at some point be able to collect some of the cost of the repairs from him. Not that I needed the money, of course.

It was more about making sure justice was served on as many levels as possible.

"Well," Josie went on, "I'm just glad to see that your shop is being fixed so quickly, and that you kept looking even after the rest of us thought Trent

Reynolds' killer was in jail. Your intuition definitely served you well this time."

And thank the Goddess for that, because I hadn't wanted to give up on my gut instincts when they'd served me so well in the past. Somehow, I should have known the universe would do its best to look out for me and the people I cared about.

As for Manuel Lorca, the murder charges against him had been dropped, but that didn't mean he was going to be getting out of jail any time soon. The drug arrest had been his third strike, so I had a feeling he would be spending quite some time behind bars.

"Oh, well," I told Josie with a deprecating lift of my shoulders. "Something just kept niggling at me."

"Good thing it did." She paused there for a moment, then added, "How is Sofia doing?"

"She's all right," I said. "Shaken up by the whole thing, obviously, but I think she's going to come out of it okay. In fact, I'm meeting her for lunch today. We have a few things we need to talk about."

"Oh?" Josie inquired, obviously hoping I would spill the beans.

But since nothing was a done deal yet, I only assumed what I hoped was an enigmatic expression and replied, "I'll let you know when I know."

She must have been able to tell I wasn't going

to offer anything more than that somewhat evasive reply, because she only commented, "Well, I guess I'll have to be satisfied with that. Good luck with your window—I have a house showing I need to get to."

Of course she did. Josie Woodrow probably could have sold a house on Christmas Day if the mood took her.

In the meantime, I hung around while the glaziers finished their job and then thanked them when they were done. Because I hadn't known for sure how long the task would take, the store was closed today as well, although we'd be open for business as usual on Wednesday, with just six days to go until Christmas.

Time enough.

Sofia stared across the table at me, expression shocked. "You want to go into business with me?"

We were sitting in Olamendi's, which was decorated with paper poinsettias and a bewildering variety of miniature Christmas trees with different themes, while "Feliz Navidad" blared from the speakers mounted high up on the walls. I'd figured it was better to meet there, both because it was closer to my shop and Hazel's Airbnb, and also because The Flatiron was the last place Sofia had eaten with Kurt before his arrest, and I didn't want the setting to dredge up any bad memories.

"Everyone says your beers are amazing," I said. "In fact, Chuck told me you missed out on the grand prize by only two points."

Her lips pursed. "That's supposed to make me feel better?"

I chuckled. "Well, more like, I wanted you to know it was a very, very close second. And a lot of people seemed very receptive to the idea of a brewpub opening here in downtown. I guess the thing is, would you be interested in doing something like that? Or would you rather stay in Flagstaff?"

Sofia didn't reply right away, and instead reached for a chip from the basket in the middle of the table and dunked it in some of Rosie, the restaurant owner's, world-famous tomatillo salsa. "I'm not married to Flagstaff, if that's what you're asking. I just moved there because it worked out with where I wanted to take my career. But maybe starting over here in Globe would be a good thing."

Her comment surprised me a little, just because up until now, Sofia had seemed almost too neutral on the subject of opening a business so far away from the place where she was currently established. But then, she was the kind of person who always seemed a little guarded, a little too quiet, as though she'd had to build up those sorts of defenses when dealing with Kurt Vonn.

He was no longer a factor in her life, though, so now she could make her decisions without having to worry about what he might say or do.

"It did wonders for me," I said with a smile. "I left L.A. almost three years ago, and my whole life changed for the better."

For just a second, Sofia's gaze slid toward my swollen midsection, not completely hidden by the table where we sat. A small quirk showed at the corner of her mouth, and I wondered what she was thinking. Had she ever planned to have a family with Kurt, or was she too focused on her career to worry about such things?

I wouldn't ask, of course, because we still didn't know each other very well. As time wore on...I'd just have to see.

"What would your terms be?" she asked next, now sounding a little hesitant. I had no idea what her business arrangement with Kurt had been, but I had to believe he'd been taking a lot more than his fair share.

But I didn't operate that way, so I thought Sofia would be pleasantly surprised. "Five percent of net until the loan's paid off," I responded, and once again, shock flickered in her clear blue eyes.

"That might take a long time," she warned me,

but I only shook my head and reached for a chip of my own.

"I'm not in any hurry," I said, hoping my casual tone would let her know I truly wasn't worried about how long it might take for her to pay me back. No, I wasn't about to divulge my net worth, but I also wanted her to understand that giving her the loan wasn't going to cause me any financial hardship. "It's more important to me that Globe has a new restaurant, because we've been dying for one...and also important for you to get the recognition you deserve."

A hopeful light shone in her eyes then. I hoped she was imagining the future I'd already imagined for her—a thriving brewpub here in the heart of Globe's downtown, a new and ever-widening circle of friends. Housing wouldn't be a problem, because I'd already checked with Hazel to see if she would be open to renting her house long-term if Sofia decided to stay here and get her business started. True, that sort of arrangement had turned out to be something of a disaster when Melanie Knowles had come to work for me, but I knew things would be different with Sofia. She was an entirely different person, and I knew I could trust her, because she was a woman who'd speak the truth even if it put her in a bad light.

"Okay," she said at length. "I'm in. What's next?"

"Well, we need Josie to show us the old hardware store to make sure it really would be suitable for your brewpub," I answered. "And after that, I'll need to have my lawyer draw up the documents. Still, I'm pretty sure we can get started after the first of the year."

"'The first of the year,'" Sofia repeated, now sounding almost dreamy, as if her mind was already filling up with all sorts of hopeful possibilities. "That works. I'll need some time to get things settled up in Flagstaff, anyway. Luckily, the house belongs to Kurt, so I suppose he'll have to deal with that."

Which probably wouldn't be a lot of fun, based on what I knew had happened to Miriam Jacobsen's house after I'd discovered she was involved in the faux haunting—and subsequent death of the demon hunter my mother had hired to investigate the phenomena—of the mansion my mother and her husband Tom had bought here in Globe. Eventually, Miriam's house had been put up for sale, since there was no way her family could afford to keep up with the payments on the place. It had all worked out for the best in the end, since Archie and Victoria had picked up the house for far less than Miriam's family had been asking, but still, dealing with a property when the owner has been sent off to prison was a hassle no matter how you looked at it.

But Kurt wouldn't be facing these complications if he hadn't decided to cold-bloodedly kill a man he viewed as a rival, so I supposed this was just the universe letting him know he'd made his own bed...and now he'd have to lie in it.

"I'll get in touch with Josie and see when she's available to show us the building," I said. "And after that—well, I suppose we'll just figure it out as we go along."

"That sounds good to me," Sofia replied.

We were both drinking water, but we picked up our glasses anyway to clink them together to seal the deal.

I'd already discussed the situation with Calvin and he'd been on board with the whole thing...even as he'd appeared a little concerned that I was biting off more than I could chew, considering the baby would be here in less than three months. But I'd assured him I was only providing the funding for the brewpub and Sofia would otherwise be managing the project, and he'd been content with that.

No, we could all relax and enjoy our holiday, and then she'd be back here to begin her new future with the new year. With any luck, the business would be up and running by summer, and the people of Globe—and its visitors—would be able to enjoy Sofia's wonderful lagers and wheat beers while reveling in the return of long, lazy days and warm, welcome nights.

We all had so much to look forward to. I smiled across the table at her, knowing that, despite the tragedies she'd just endured, she could soon look forward to her own time in the sun.

The Hedgewitch for Hire series will conclude in *Charm School,* releasing in July 2024.

FAMILIAR SPIRITS

(Cozy Mystery/Paranormal Romance)

Spells and Spaniels

Cauldrons and Cats

Hexes and Hedgehogs

Charms and Chihuahuas

Runes and Ravens (September 2024)

LATTES AND LEVITATION*

(Cozy Mystery/Paranormal Romance)

Caffeine Before Curses

Muffins After Magic

Pastries and Prophecies

Eclairs and Ectoplasm

Sugar Skulls and Specters

Wedding Cakes and Wishes

HEDGEWITCH FOR HIRE

(Cozy Mystery/Paranormal Romance)

Grave Mistake

Social Medium

Household Demons

Perpetual Potion

Jingle Spells

Wandering Monsters

Uninvited Ghosts

Prophet Motive

Ballroom Bits

Spell Check

Brew Confessions

Charm School (July 2024)

UNEXPECTED MAGIC*

(Urban Fantasy/Paranormal Romance)

Found Objects

Finders, Keepers

Lost and Found

Finding Destiny

THE WITCHES OF WHEELER PARK*

(Paranormal Romance)

Storm Born

Thunder Road

Winds of Change

Mind Games

A Wheeler Park Christmas

Blood Ties

Healing Hands

Wishful Thinking

Smoke and Mirrors

MISS PRIMM'S ACADEMY FOR WAYWARD
WITCHES*

(Fantasy/Academy Romance)

Misspelled

Dispelled

Expelled

PROJECT DEMON HUNTERS*

(Paranormal Romance)

Unquiet Souls

Unbound Spirits

Unholy Ground

Unseen Voices

Unmarked Graves

Unbroken Vows

THE DEVIL YOU KNOW*

(Paranormal Romance)

Sympathy for the Devil

Charmed, I'm Sure

Λ Wing and a Prayer

Wish Upon a Star

THE WITCHES OF CANYON ROAD*

(Paranormal Romance)

Hidden Gifts

Darker Paths

Mysterious Ways

A Canyon Road Christmas

Demon Born

An Ill Wind

Higher Ground

Haunted Hearts

THE WITCHES OF CLEOPATRA HILL*

(Paranormal Romance)

Darkangel

Darknight

Darkmoon

Sympathetic Magic

Protector

Spellbound

A Cleopatra Hill Christmas

Impractical Magic

Strange Magic

The Arrangement

Defender

Bad Blood

Deep Magic

Darktide

THE WATCHERS TRILOGY*

(Paranormal Romance)

Falling Dark

Dead of Night

Rising Dawn

THE SEDONA FILES*

(Paranormal/Science Fiction Romance)

Bad Vibrations

Desert Hearts

Angel Fire

Star Crossed

Falling Angels

Enemy Mine

TALES OF THE LATTER KINGDOMS*

(Fantasy Romance)

All Fall Down

Dragon Rose

Binding Spell

Ashes of Roses

One Thousand Nights

Threads of Gold

The Wolf of Harrow Hall

Moon Dance

The Song of the Thrush

THE GAIAN CONSORTIUM SERIES*

(Science Fiction Romance)

Beast (free prequel novella)

Blood Will Tell

Breath of Life

The Gaia Gambit

The Mandala Maneuver

The Titan Trap

The Zhore Deception

The Refugee Ruse

STANDALONE TITLES

Hearts on Fire (Paranormal Romance)

Taking Dictation (Contemporary Romance)

Golden Heart (Gaslight Fantasy Romance)

Night Music: A Modern Reimagining of The Phantom
of the Opera (Contemporary Romance)

Ghost Dance: A Sequel to Gaston Leroux's The
Phantom of the Opera (Historical Mystery/Romance)

Flight Before Christmas (Fantasy Romance)

* Indicates a completed series

About the Author

USA *Today* bestselling author Christine Pope has been writing stories ever since she commandeered her family's Smith-Corona typewriter back in grade school. Her work includes paranormal romance, cozy paranormal mystery, and urban fantasy, among others. She makes her home in New Mexico.

Christine Pope on the Web:
www.christinepope.com

facebook.com/ChristinePopeAuthor

pinterest.com/ChristineJPope

bookbub.com/authors/christine-pope